THE CARBONELS

THE CARBONELS

Charlotte M. Yonge

WILDSIDE PRESS

The Carbonels

For more information, contact:
www.wildsidepress.com

CHAPTER I.

French Measure.

"For thy walls a pretty slight drollery."
The Second Part of King Henry IV.

"A bad lot. Yes, sir, a thoroughly bad lot."

"You don't mean it."

"Yes, ma'am, a bad lot is the Uphill people. Good for nothing and ungrateful! I've known them these thirty-years, and no one will do anything with them."

The time was the summer of 1822. The place was a garden, somewhat gone to waste, with a gravel drive running round a great circle of periwinkles with a spotted aucuba in the middle. There was a low, two-storied house, with green shutters, green Venetian blinds, and a rather shabby verandah painted in alternate stripes of light and darker green. In front stood a high gig, with a tall old, bony horse trying to munch the young untrimmed shoots of a lilac in front of him as he waited for the speaker, a lawyer, dressed as country attorneys were wont to dress in those days, in a coat of invisible green, where the green constantly became more visible, brown trousers, and under them drab gaiters. He was addressing a gentleman in a blue coat and nankeen trousers, but evidently military, and two ladies in white dresses, narrow as to the skirts, but full in the sleeves. One had a blue scarf over her shoulders and blue ribbons in her very large Leghorn bonnet; the other had the same in green, and likewise a green veil. Her bonnet was rather more trimmed, the dress more embroidered, the scarf of a richer, broader material than the other's, and it was thus evident that she was the married sister; but they were a good deal alike, with the same wholesome smooth complexion, brown eyes, and hair in great shining rolls under their bonnet caps, much the same pleasant expression, and the same neat little feet in crossed sandalled shoes and white stockings showing out beneath their white tambour-worked gowns.

With the above verdict, the lawyer made his parting bow, and drove off along a somewhat rough road through two pasture fields. The first gate, white and ornamental, was held open for him by an old man in a short white smock and long leathern gaiters, the second his own servant opened, the third was held by half a dozen shock-headed children, with their backs against it and hands held out, but in vain; he only smacked his driving-whip over their heads, and though he did not strike any of them, they requited it with a prolonged yell, which reached the ears of the trio in front of the house.

"I'm afraid it is not far from the truth," said the green lady.

"Oh no; I am sure he is a horrid man," said her blue sister. "I would not believe him for a moment."

"Only with a qualification," rejoined the gentleman.

"But, Edmund, couldn't you be sure that it is just what he would say, whatever the people were?"

"I am equally sure that the exaction of rents is not the way to see people at their best."

"Come in, come in! We have all our settling in to do, and no time for you two to fight."

Edmund, Mary, Dorothea, and Sophia Carbonel were second cousins, who had always known one another in the house of the girls' father, a clergyman in a large country town. Edmund had been in the army just in time for the final battles of the Peninsular war, and had since served with the army of occupation and in Canada. He had always meant that Mary should be his wife, but the means were wanting to set up housekeeping, until the death of an old uncle of his mother's made him heir to Greenhow Farm, an estate bringing in about 500 pounds a year. Mary and her next sister Dora had in the meantime lost their parents, and had been living with some relations in London, where their much younger sister Sophy was at school, until Edmund, coming home, looked over the farm, decided that it would be a fit home for the sisters, and retired from the army forthwith. Thus then, after a brief tour among the Lakes, they had taken up Dora in London, and here they were; Sophy was to join them when the holidays began. Disorder reigned indeed within, and hammers resounded, nor was the passage easy among the packing-cases that encumbered the narrow little vestibule whence the stairs ascended.

Under the verandah were the five sash windows of the three front rooms, the door, of course, in the middle. Each had a little shabby furniture, to which the Carbonels were adding, and meant to add more; the dining-room had already been papered with red flock in stripes, the drawing-room with a very delicate white, on which were traced in tender colouring-baskets of vine leaves and laburnums.

Dora gave a little scream. "Look! Between the windows, Mary; see, the laburnums and grapes are hanging upward."

"Stupid people!" exclaimed Mary, "I see. Happily, it is only on that one piece, but how Edmund will be vexed."

"Perhaps there is another piece unused."

"I am sure I hope there is! Don't you know, Edmund fell in love with it at Paris. It was his first provision for future house-keeping, and it was lying laid up in lavender all these years till we were ready for it."

"It is only that one division, which is a comfort."

"What's the matter?" and the master of the house came in.

"Senseless beings! It must be covered directly. It is a desight to the whole room. Here!" and he went out to the carpenter, who was universal builder to the village, and was laying down the stair carpet. "Here, Hewlett, do you see what you have done?"

Hewlett, a large man with a smooth, plump, but honest face, came in, in his shirt sleeves, apron, and paper cap, touched his forehead to the ladies, stood, and stared.

"Can't you see?" sharply demanded the captain.

Hewlett scratched his head, and gazed round.

"See here! How do grapes grow? Or laburnums?"

An idea broke in on him.

"What! they be topsy-turvy?" he slowly observed, after looking from the faulty breadth to the next.

"Of course they are. Find the rest of the paper! We must have a piece put on at once, or the whole appearance of the room is spoilt," said Captain Carbonel. "It will make a delay, but it must be done at once. Where is the piece left over?"

Hewlett retreated to find it, while the captain said something about "stupid ass."

Presently his gruff voice was heard demanding, "Dan, I say, where's the remnant of that there fancy paper?"

Dan's answer did not rise into audible words, but presently Hewlett tramped back, saying, "There ain't none, sir."

"I tell you there must be," returned the captain, in the same angry tones. And he proceeded to show that the number of pieces he had bought, and the measure of which he had ascertained, was such that there ought to have been half-a-piece left over from papering the room, the size of which he had exactly taken. Hewlett could do nothing but stolidly repeat that "there weren't none left, not enow to make a mouse's nest."

"Who did the papering? Did you?"

"Daniel Hewlett, sir, he did the most on it. My cousin, sir."

The captain fell upon Daniel, who had more words at command, but was equally strong in denial of having any remnant. "They had only skimped out enough," he said, "just enough for the walls, and it was a close fit anyhow."

The captain loudly declared it impossible, but Mary ran out in the midst to suggest that mayhap the defect was in the French measure. Each piece might not have been the true number of whatever they called them in that new revolutionary fashion.

Dan Hewlett's face cleared up. "Ay, 'tis the French measure, sure, sir. Of course they can't do nothing true and straight! I be mortal sorry the ladies is disappointed, but it bain't no fault of mine, sir."

"And look here, Edmund," continued Mary, "it will not spoil the room at all if Mr. Hewlett will help move the tall bureau against it, and we'll hang the 'Death of General Wolfe' above it, and then there won't be more than two bits of laburnum to be seen, even if you are curious enough to get upon a chair to investigate."

"Well, it must be so," returned Captain Carbonel, "but I hate the idea of makeshifts and having imperfections concealed."

"Just like you, Edmund," laughed Dora. "You will always seem to be looking right through at the upright sprays, though all the solid weight of Hume, Gibbon, and Rollin is in front of them."

"Precisely," said Edmund. "It is not well to feel that there is anything to be hidden. The chief part of the vexation is, however," he added — shutting the door and lowering his voice — "that I am convinced that there must have been foul play somewhere."

"Oh, Edmund; French measure!"

"Nonsense! That does not account for at least a whole piece disappearing."

He took out a pencil, and went again into his calculations, while his sister-in-law indignantly exclaimed —

"It is all prejudice, because that horrid attorney said all these poor people were a bad lot."

"Hush, hush!" said Mrs. Carbonel, rather frightened, and —

"I advise you to think before you speak," said Captain Carbonel quietly but sternly.

Still Dora could not help saying, as soon as she was alone with her sister, "I shall believe in the French measure. I like that slow, dull man, and I am sure he is honest."

"Yes, dear, only pray don't say any more to Edmund, but let us get the bookcase placed as fast as we can, and let him forget all about it."

CHAPTER II.

The Lie of the Land.

"Thank you, pretty cow, that gave
Pleasant milk to soak my bread,
Every day and every night
Warm and fresh, and sweet and bright."
J. Taylor.

Darkness had descended before there had been time to do more than shake into the downstair rooms and bedrooms and be refreshed with the evening meal, but with morning began the survey of the new home.

The front part of the house had three living rooms, with large sash windows, almost to the ground, shaded by the verandah. These were drawing-room, dining-room, and study, the last taken out of the entry, where was the staircase, and there were three similar rooms above. These had been added by the late owner to the original farmhouse, with a fine old-fashioned kitchen that sent Mary and Dora into greater raptures than their cook. There were offices around, a cool dairy, where stood great red glazed pans of delicious-looking cream and milk, and a clean white wooden churn that Dora longed to handle. The farmhouse rooms were between it and the new ones, and there were a good many rooms above, the red-tiled roof rising much higher than that of the more modern part of the house. There was a narrow paling in front, and then came the farmyard, enclosed in barns, cow-houses and cart-sheds, and a cottage where the bailiff, Master Pucklechurch, had taken up his abode, having hitherto lived in the farmhouse. He was waiting to show Captain Carbonel over the farm. He was a grizzled, stooping old fellow, with a fine, handsome, sunburnt face; bright, shrewd, dark eyes looking out between puckers, a short white smock-frock, and long gaiters. It was not their notion of a bailiff but the lawyer, who was so chary of his praise, had said that old Master Pucklechurch and his wife were absolutely trustworthy. They had managed the farm in the interregnum, and brought him weekly accounts in their heads, for neither could write, with the most perfect regularity and minuteness. And his face did indeed bespeak confidence in his honesty, as he touched his hat in answer to the greeting.

The ladies, however, looked and smelt in some dismay, for the centre of the yard was a mountain of manure and straw, with a puce-coloured pond beside it. On the summit of the mountain a handsome ruddy cock, with a splendid dark-green arched tail, clucked, chuckled, and scratched for his speckled, rose-crowned hens, a green-headed, curly-tailed drake "steered forth his fleet upon the lake" of brown ducks and their yellow progeny, and pigs of the plum-pudding order rooted in the intermediate regions. The road which led to the cart-sheds and to the house, skirted round this unsavoury tract.

"Oh, Edmund!" sighed Mary.

"Farmer's wife, Mary," said her husband, smiling. "It ought to be a perfect nosegay to you."

"I'm sure it is not wholesome," she said, looking really distressed, and he dropped his teasing tone, and said —

"Of course it shall be remedied! I will see to it."

A dismal screeching and cackling here attracted the attention of the sisters, who started towards Pucklechurch's cottage, and the fowl-house, (a very foul house by the by) in front of which, on a low wooden stool, sat a tidy old woman, Betty Pucklechurch in fact, in a tall muslin cap, spotted kerchief blue gown, and coarse apron, with a big girl before her holding the unfortunate hen, whose cries had startled them.

"Oh, don't go near! She is killing it," cried Dora.

"No;" as the hen, with a final squawk, shook out her ruffled feathers, and rushed away to tell her woes to her companions on the dunghill, while the old woman jumped up, smoothed down her apron, and curtsied low.

"What were you doing?" asked Mary, still startled.

"Only whipping her breast with nettles, ma'am, to teach her to sit close in her nest, the plaguey thing, and not be gadding after the rest."

"Poor thing!" cried Dora. "But oh, look, look, Mary, at the

dear little chickens!"

They were in the greatest delight at the three broods of downy little chickens, and one of ducklings, whose parent hens were clucking in coops; and in the kitchen they found a sickly one nursed in flannel in a basket, and an orphaned lamb which staggered upon its disproportionate black legs at sight of Betty.

"Ay! he be always after me," she said. "They terrify one terrible, as if 'twas their mother, till they can run with the rest."

Dora would have petted the lamb, but it retreated from her behind Betty's petticoats, and she could only listen to Mary's questions about how much butter was made from how many cows milk, and then be taken to see the two calves, one of which Betty pronounced to be "but a staggering Bob yet, but George Butcher would take he in a sen'night," which sounded so like senate, that it set Dora wondering what council was to pronounce on the fate of the poor infant bull.

Over his stall, Edmund found them, after an inspection of the pig-styes, and having much offended Master Pucklechurch by declaring that he would have them kept clean, and the pigs no longer allowed to range about the yard.

"Bless you, sir, the poor things would catch their death of cold and die," was the answer to the one edict; and to the other, "They'd never take to their victuals, nor fat kindly without their range first."

"Then let them have it in the home-field out there, where I see plenty of geese."

"They'll spile every bit of grass, sir," was the growling objection; and still worse was the suggestion, which gradually rose into a command, that the "muck-heap" should be removed to the said home-field, and never allowed to accumulate in such close proximity to the house.

Pucklechurch said little; but his "If it be your will, sir," sounded like a snarl, and after ruminating for some time, he brought out — as if it were an answer to a question about the team of horses —

"We'll have to take on another boy, let be a man, if things is to be a that 'en a."

"Let us, then," said the captain, and joined his ladies, with the old man depressed and grumbling inwardly.

There was an orchard preparing to be beautiful with blossom, and a considerable kitchen garden at the back and on the other side of the house, bounded by an exceedingly dirty and be-rutted farm road, over which the carriage had jolted the evening before. The extensive home-field in front was shut off from the approach by a belt of evergreens, and sloped slightly upwards towards the hill which gave the parish its name.

"We will cut off a nice carriage road," said Mary, as she looked at it.

"All in good time," replied her husband, not wishing further to shock poor Master Pucklechurch, who had to conduct the party to the arable fields — one of which was being ploughed by three fine sleek horses, led by Bill Morris, with his father at the shafts. In another, their approach was greeted by hideous yells and shouts which made Dora start.

"Ay, ay," said Pucklechurch, "he knows how to holler when he see me a-coming;" and at the same time a black-specked cloud of rooks rose up from the furrows, the old man stamping towards the boy who ought to have been keeping them, vituperating him in terms that it was as well not to hear.

And it was such a tiny boy after all, and in such a pair of huge boots with holes showing his bare toes. However, they served him to run away from Master Pucklechurch into the furthest ditch, and if the ladies had designs on him, they had to be deferred.

On the opposite side were more fields, with crops in various stages, one lovely with the growing wheat and barley, another promising potatoes, and another beans; and beyond, towards the river, were meadows parted by broad hedgerows, with paths between, in which a few primroses and golden celandines looked up beneath the withy buds and the fluttering hazel catkins. Then came the meadows, in one of which fed the cows, pretty buff-and-white creatures, and in another field were hurdled the sheep, among their dole of turnips, sheep and turnips alike emitting an odour of the most unpleasant kind, and the deep baas of the ewes, and the thinner wail of the lambs made a huge mass of sounds; while Captain Carbonel tried to talk to Master Buttermere the shepherd, a silent, crusty, white-haired old man in a green smock and grey old coat, who growled out scarcely a word.

So the tour of the property was made, and old Pucklechurch expressed his opinion. "He'll never make nothing of it; he is too outlandish and full of his fancies, and his madam's a fine lady. 'Pon my word and honour, she was frought at that there muck-heap!"

This pleasant augury was of course not known to the newcomers, who found something so honest and worthy about the Pucklechurches that they could not help liking them, though Mrs. Carbonel had another tussle with Betty about fresh butter. "It war no good to make it more than once a week. Folk liked it tasty and meller;" and that the Carbonels had by no means the same likings, made her hold up her hands and agree with her husband that their failure was certain. These first few days were spent in the needful arrangements of house and furniture, during which time Captain Carbonel came to the conclusion that no one could be more stupid or awkward than Master Hewlett, but that he was an honest man, and tried to do his best, such as it was, while his relation, Dan, though cleverer, was much more slippery, and could not be depended upon. Dora asked Master Hewlett what schools there were in the place, and he made answer that the little ones went in to Dame Verdon, but she didn't make much of it, not since she had had the shaking palsy, and she could not give the lads the stick. He thought of sending his biggest lad to school at Poppleby next spring, but 'twas a long way, and his good woman didn't half like it, not unless there was some one going the same way.

Betty Pucklechurch's account amounted to much the same. "Dame Verdon had had the school nigh about forty years. She had taught them all to read their Testament, all as stayed long enough, for there was plenty for the children to do; and folks said she wasn't up to hitting them as she used to be."

Farmer Goodenough, the churchwarden, who came to see Captain Carbonel about the letting of a field which was mixed up with the Greenhow property, gave something of the like character. "She is getting old, certain sure, but she is a deserving woman, and she keeps off the parish."

"But can she teach the children?"

"She can teach them all they need to know, and keep the little ones out of mischief," said the farmer, perhaps beginning to be alarmed. "No use to learn them no more. What do they want of it for working in the fields or milking the cows?"

"They ought at least to know their duty to God and their neighbour," said Captain Carbonel. "Is there no Sunday School?"

"No, sir," — very bluntly. "I hear talk of such things at Poppleby and the like," he added, "but we don't want none of them here. The lot here are quite bad enough, without maggots being put into their heads."

Captain Carbonel did not wish to continue the subject. The farmer's own accent did not greatly betoken acquaintance with schools of any sort.

Of course the wife and sister were amused as well as saddened by his imitative account of the farmer's last speech, but they meant to study the subject on their first Sunday. They had learnt already that Uphill Priors was a daughter church to Downhill Priors, and had only one service on a Sunday, alternate mornings and evenings. The vicar was the head of a house at Oxford, and only came to the parsonage in the summer. The services were provided for by a curate, living at Downhill, with the assistance of the master of a private school, to whom the vicarage was let. When Captain Carbonel asked Master Pucklechurch about the time, he answered, "Well, sir, 'tis morning churching. So it will be half-past ten, or else eleven, or else no time at all."

"What, do you mean that there will be none?"

"No, sir. There will be churching sure enough, but just as time may chance, not to call it an hour. Best way is to start as soon as you sights the parson a-coming past the gate down there. Then you're sure to be in time. Bell strikes out as soon as they sees him beyond the 'Prior's Lane.'"

The Carbonels, in Sunday trim, with William the man-servant, and two maids, their Prayerbooks in white pocket-hand-kerchiefs, following in the rear, set forth for the gate, in the spring freshness. The grass in the fields was beginning to grow up, the hedges were sprouting with tender greens and reds, the polished stems of the celandine were opening to the sunshine in the banks, with here and there a primrose. Birds were singing all round, and a lark overhead — most delightful plea-sures to those so long shut up in a town. It was the side of a hill, where the fields were cut out into most curious forms, probably to suit the winding of a little brook or the shape of the ground; and there were, near the bottom, signs of a mass of daffodils, which filled the sisters with delight, though daffodils were not then the fashion, and were rather despised as yellow and scentless.

As they came near the second gate, they saw a black figure go by on an old white horse; then they came out on a long ascending lane with deep ruts, bordered by fresh soft turf on either sides, with hawthorn hedges, and at intervals dark yew trees.

A cracked bell struck up, by which they understood that the clergyman had come in sight, and they came themselves out upon a village green, where geese, donkeys, and boys in greenish smock-frocks, seemed to be all mixed up together. Thatched cottages stood round the green, and a public-house — the "Fox and Hounds." The sign consisted of a hunt, elaborately cut out in tin, huntsman, dogs, and fox, rushing across from the inn on a high uplifted rod of iron, fastened into a pole on the further side of the road, whence the sound of the bell proceeded, and whither the congregation in smock-frocks and black bonnets were making their way.

Following in this direction, the Carbonels, much amused, passed under the hunt, went some distance further, and found a green churchyard, quite shut in by tall elm trees, which, from the road, almost hid the tiny tumble-down church, from whose wooden belfry the call proceeded. It really seemed to be buried in the earth, and the little side windows looked out into a ditch. There were two steps to go down into the deep porch, and within there seemed to be small space between the roof and the top of the high square pew into which they were ushered by Master Hewlett, who, it seemed, was the parish clerk.

They saw little from it, but on one side, hung from the roof a huge panel with the royal arms, painted in the reign of William and Mary, as the initials in the corners testified, and with the lion licking his lips most comically; on the other side was a great patch of green damp; behind, a gallery, full of white smock-frocked men with their knees thrust through the rails in front. Immediately before them rose the tall erection of pulpit, the fusty old cushion and tassels, each faded to a different tint, overhanging so much that Dora could not help thinking that a thump from an energetic preacher would send it down on Edmund's head in a cloud of dust. There was the reading-desk below, whence the edges of a ragged Prayer-book protruded, and above it presently appeared a very full but much-frayed surplice, and a thin worn face between white whiskers. The service was quietly and reverently read, but not a response seemed to come from anywhere except from Master Hewlett's powerful lungs, somewhere in the rear, and there was a certain murmur of chattering in the chancel followed by a resounding whack. Then Master Hewlett's head was seen, and his steps heard as he tramped along the aisle and climbed up the gallery stairs, as the General Thanksgiving began, and there he shouted out the number of the Psalm, "new version," that is, from Brady and Tate, which every one had bound up with the Prayer-book. Then a bassoon brayed, and a fiddle squealed, and the Psalm resounded with hearty goodwill and better tone than could have been expected.

Master Hewlett stayed to assist in the second singing, and the children, who sat on low forms and on the chancel step, profited by it to make their voices more audible than the Commandments, though the clergyman had not gone to the altar, and once in the course of the sermon, Captain Carbonel was impelled to stand up and look over the edge of the pew, when he beheld a battle royal going on over a length of string, between a boy in a blue petticoat and one in a fustian jacket. At the unwonted sight, the fustian-clad let go, and blue petticoat tumbled over backwards, kicking up a great pair of red legs, grey socks, and imperfect but elephantine boots, and howling at the same time. The preacher stopped short, the clerk had by this time worked his way down from the gallery, and, collaring both the antagonists, hauled them out into the churchyard, the triple stamping being heard on the pavement all the way. The sermon was resumed and read to its conclusion. It was a very good one, but immensely beyond the capacity of the congregation, and Mary Carbonel had a strong suspicion that she had heard it before.

It was only on coming out that any notion could be gathered of the congregation. There were a good many men and big boys, in smocks, a few green, but most of them beautifully white and embroidered; their wearers had sat without books through the whole service, and now came out with considerable trampling.

The pews contained the young girls in gorgeous colours, the old women, and the better class of people, but not many of them, for the "petit noblesse" of Uphill were very "petit" indeed, in means and numbers; but their bonnets were enormous, and had red or purple bows standing upright on them, and the farmers had drab coats and long gaiters. The old dames curtsied low, the little girls stared, and the boys peeped out from behind the slanting old headstones and grinned. Some of them had been playing at marbles on the top of the one square old monument, until routed by Master Hewlett on his coming out with the two combatants.

Captain Carbonel had gone round to the vestry door to make acquaintance with the clergyman, though Farmer Goodenough informed him in an audible whisper, "He ain't the right one, sir; he be only schoolmaster."

And when the two met at the door, and the captain shook hands and said that they would be neighbours, he was received with a certain hesitating smile.

"I should tell you, sir, that I am only taking occasional duty here — assisting. I am Mr. Atkins. I have a select private academy at the vicarage, which the President of Saint Cyril's lets to me. He is here in the summer holidays."

"I understand. The curate lives at Downhill!" said Captain

Carbonel.

"At the priory, in fact, with his father's family. Yes, it is rather an unfortunate state of affairs," he said, answering the captain's countenance rather than his words; "but I have no responsibility. I merely assist in the Sunday duty; and, indeed, I advise you to have as little to do with the Uphill people as possible. An idle good-for-nothing set! Any magistrate would tell you that there's no parish where they have so many up before them."

"No wonder!" said Captain Carbonel under his breath.

"A bad set," repeated Mr. Atkins, pausing at the shed where his old grey horse was put up; and there they parted.

The captain and his wife and her sister walked to Downhill, two miles off, across broad meadows, a river, and a pretty old bridge, the next Sunday morning, found the church scantily filled, but with more respectable-looking people, and heard the same sermon over again, so that Mary was able to identify it with one in a published volume.

CHAPTER III.

The Turnip Field.

"You ask me why the poor complain,
And these have answered thee."
Southey.

"Hullo, Molly Hewlett, who'd ha' thought of seeing you out here?"

It was in a wet turnip field, and a row of women were stooping over it, picking out the weeds. The one that was best off had great boots, a huge weight to carry in themselves; but most had them sadly torn and broken. Their skirts, of no particular colour, were tucked up, and they had either a very old man's coat, or a smock-frock cut short, or a small old woollen shawl, which last left the blue and red arms bare; on their heads were the oldest of bonnets, or here and there a sun-bonnet, which looked more decent. One or two babies were waiting in the hedgeside in the charge of little girls.

"Molly Hewlett," exclaimed another of the set, straightening herself up. "Why, I thought your Dan was working with Master Hewlett, for they Gobblealls," (which was what Uphill made of Carbonel).

"So he be; but what is a poor woman to do when more than half his wage goes to the 'Fox and Hounds,' and she has five children to keep and my poor sister, not able to do a turn? There's George Hewlett, grumbling and growling at him too, and no one knows how long he'll keep him on."

"What! George, his cousin, as was bound to keep him on?"

"I don't know; George is that particular himself, and them new folks, Gobbleall as they call them, are right down mean, and come down on you if they misses one little mossle of parkisit; and there's my poor sister to keep — as is afflicted, and can't do nothing!"

"But she pays you handsome," said Betsy Seddon, "and looks after the children besides."

"Pays, indeed! Not half enough to keep her, with all the trouble of helping her about! Not that I grudges it, but she wants things extry, you see, and Dan he don't like it. But no doubt the ladies will take notice of her."

"I thought the lady kind enough," interposed another woman. "She noticed how lame our granny was with the rheumatics, and told me to send up for broth."

"We wants somewhat bad enough," returned another thin woman, with her hand to her side. "Nobody never does nothing for no one here!"

"Nor we don't want no one to come worriting and terrifying," cried the last of the group, with fierce black eyes and rusty black hair sticking out beyond her man's beaver hat, tied on with a yellow handkerchief. "Always at one about church and school, and meddling with everything — the ribbon on one's bonnet and to the very pots on the fire. I knows what they be like in Tydeby! And what do you get by it, but old cast clothes and broth made of dish-washings?" She enforced all this with more than one word not to be written.

"I know, I'd be thankful for that!" murmured the thin woman, who looked as if she had barely a petticoat on, and could have had scarcely a breakfast.

"Oh, we all know's Bessy Mole is all for what she can get!" said the independent woman, tossing her head.

"And had need to be," returned Molly Hewlett, in a scornful tone, which made the poor woman in question stoop all the lower, and pull her groundsel more diligently.

"The broth ain't bad," ventured she who had tried it.

"I shall see what I can get out of them," added another. "I bain't proud; and my poor children's shoes is a shame to see."

"You'll not get much," said Molly Hewlett, with a sniff. "the captain, as they calls him, come down on my Jem, as was taking home a little bit of a chip for the fire, and made him put it down, as cross as could be."

"How now, you lazy, trolloping, gossiping women! What are you after?"

Farmer Goodenough was upon them; and the words he showered on them were not by any means "good enough" to be repeated here. He stormed at them for their idleness so furiously as to set off the babies in the hedge screaming and yelling. Tirzah Todd, the gipsy-looking woman whom he especially abused, tossed her head and marched off in the midst, growling fiercely, to quiet her child; and he, sending a parting imprecation after her, directed his violence upon poor Bessy Mole, though all this time she had been creeping on, shaking, trembling, and crying, under the pelting of the storm; but, unluckily, in her nervousness and blindness from tears, she pulled up a young turnip, and the farmer fell on her and rated her hotly for not being worth half her wage, and doing him more harm than good with her carelessness. She had not a word to say for herself, and went on shivering and trying to check her sobs while he shouted out that he only employed her from charity, and she had better look out, or he should turn her off at once.

"Oh, sir, don't!" then came out with a burst of tears. "My poor children — "

"Don't go whining about your children, but let me see you do your work."

However, this last sentence was in a milder tone, as if the fit of passion had exhausted itself; and Mr. Goodenough found his way back to the path that crossed the fields, and went on. Tirzah Todd set her teeth, clenched her fist and shook it after him, while the other women, as soon as he was out of sight, began to console Bessy Mole, who was crying bitterly and saying, "what would become of her poor children, and her own poor father."

"Never you mind, Bessy," said Molly Hewlett, "every one knows as how old Goodenough's bark is worse than his bite."

"He runs out and it's over," put in Betsy Seddon.

"I'm sure I can hardly keep about any way," sobbed the widow. "My inside is all of a quake. I can't abide words."

"Ten to one he don't give you another sixpence a week, after all," added Nanny Barton.

"He ain't no call to run out at one," said Tirzah, standing upright and flourishing her baby.

"I'd like to give him as good as he gave, an old foul-mouthed brute!"

"Look there! There's the ladies coming," exclaimed Nanny Barton.

"I thought there was some reason why he stopped his jaw so soon," exclaimed Molly, stooping down and pulling up weeds (including turnips) with undiscerning energy, in which all the others followed her example, except Tirzah, who sulkily retreated under the hedge with her baby, while Jem Hewlett and Lizzie Seddon ran forward for better convenience of staring. It was a large field, and the party were still a good way off; but as it sloped downwards behind the women, the farmer must have seen them a good deal before the weeders had done so.

These, be it remembered, were days when both farmers and their labourers were a great deal rougher in their habits than we, their grandchildren, can remember them; and there was, besides, the Old Poor Law, which left the amount of relief and of need to be fixed at the vestry meetings by the ratepayers themselves of each parish alone so that the poor were entirely dependent on the goodwill or judgment of their employers, whose minds were divided between keeping down the wages and the rates, and who had little of real principle or knowledge to guide them. It was possible to have recourse to the magistrates at the Petty Sessions, who could give an order which would override the vestry; but it was apt to be only the boldest, and often the least deserving, who could make out the best apparent cases for themselves, that ventured on such a measure.

The two ladies stopped and spoke to Molly Hewlett and Nanny Barton, whom they had seen at their doors, and who curtsied low; and Nanny, as she saw Mrs. Carbonel's eyes fall on her boots, put in —

"Yes, ma'am, 'tis bitter hard work this cold, damp weather, and wears out one's shoes ter'ble. These be an old pair of my man's, and hurts my poor feet dreadful, all over broken chilblains as they be; and my fingers, too," she added, spreading out some fingers the colour of beetroot, with dirty rags rolled round two of them.

Dora shrank. "And you can go on weeding with them?"

"Yes, ma'am. What can us do, when one's man gets but seven shillings a week. And I've had six children, and buried three," and her face looked ready for tears.

"Well, we will come and see you, and try to find something to help you," said Mrs. Carbonel. "Where do you live?"

"Out beyond the church, ma'am — a long way for a lady."

"Oh, we are good walkers."

"And please, my lady," now said Molly, coming to the front, "if you could give me an old bit of a pelisse, or anything, to make up for my boy there. He's getting big, you see, and he is terrible bad off for clothes. I don't know what is to be done for the lot of 'em."

Dora had recognised in the staring boy, who had come up close, him who had made the commotion in church; and she ventured to say, "I remember him. Don't you think, if you or his father kept him with you in church, he would behave better there?"

"Bless you, miss, his father is a sceptic. I can't go while I've got no clothes — nothing better than this, miss; and I always was used to go decent and respectable. Besides, I couldn't nohow take he into the seat with me, as Master Pucklechurch would say I was upsetting of his missus."

"Well, I hope to see him behave better next Sunday."

"Do you hear, Jem? The lady is quite shocked at your rumbustiousness! But 'twas all Joe Saunders's fault, ma'am, a terrifying the poor children. His father will give him the stick, that he will, if he hears of it again."

Meantime Mrs. Carbonel had turned to Widow Mole, who, after her first curtsey, had been weeding away diligently and coughing.

"Where do you live?" she asked. "I don't think I have seen you before."

"No, ma'am," she said quietly. "I live down the Black Hollow."

"You don't look well. Have you been ill? You have a bad cough."

"It ain't nothing, ma'am, thank you. I can keep about well enough."

"Do you take anything for it?"

"A little yarb tea at night sometimes, ma'am."

"We will try and bring you some mixture for it," said Mrs. Carbonel. And then she spoke to Betsy Seddon, who for a wonder had no request on her tongue, and asked her who the other woman was, in the hedge with the baby.

"That's Tirzah Todd, ma'am," began Mrs. Seddon, but Molly Hewlett thrust her aside, and went on, being always the most ready with words; "she is Reuben Todd's wife, and I wouldn't wish to say no harm of her, but she comes of a gipsy lot, and hasn't never got into ways that us calls reverend, though I wouldn't be saying no harm of a neighbour, ma'am."

"No, you'd better not," exclaimed a voice, for Tirzah was nearer or had better ears than Mrs. Daniel Hewlett had suspected, "though I mayn't go hypercriting about and making tales of my neighbours, as if you hadn't got a man what ain't to be called sober twice a week."

"Hush! hush!" broke in Mrs. Carbonel; "we don't want to hear all this. I hope no one will tell us unkind things of our new neighbours, for we want to be friends with all of you, especially with that bright-eyed baby. How old is it?"

She made it smile by nodding to it, and Tirzah was mollified enough to say, "Four months, ma'am; but she have a tooth coming."

"What's her name?"

Tirzah showed her pretty white teeth in a smile. "Well, ma'am, my husband he doth want to call her Jane, arter his mother, 'cause 'tis a good short name, but I calls her Hoglah, arter my sister as died."

"Then she hasn't been christened?"

"No. You see we couldn't agree, nor get gossips; and that there parson, he be always in such a mighty hurry, or I'd a had her half-baptized Hoglah, and then Reuben he couldn't hinder it."

Tirzah was getting quite confidential to Mrs. Carbonel, and Dora meantime was talking to Molly Hewlett, but here it occurred to the former that they must not waste the women's time, and they wished them good-bye, Dora fearing, however, that there would be a quarrel between Tirzah and Molly.

"Oh dear! oh dear!" she sighed, "couldn't you make peace between those two," she said; "they will fight it out."

"No, I think the fear of the farmer and the need of finishing their work will avert the storm for the present at least," said Mary, "and I thought the more I said, the worse accusations I should hear."

"But what people they are! I do begin to believe that attorney man, that they are a bad lot."

"Don't be disheartened, Dora, no one has tried yet, apparently, to do anything for them. We must try to see them in their own homes."

"Beginning with Mrs. Seddon. She was quiet and civil, and did not beg."

"Neither did that thin little woman. I should like to give her a flannel petticoat. There is a look of want about her."

"But I'm most taken with the wild woman, with the teeth and the eyes, and the merry smile. I am sure there is fun in her."

"Little enough fun, poor things!" sighed Mrs. Carbonel.

She was more used to poor people. She had more resolution, though less enthusiasm than her sister.

CHAPTER IV.

Nobody's Business.

"For the rector don't live on his living like other Christian
sort of folks."
— *T. Hood.*

The sisters found on coming home that a very handsome
chestnut horse was being walked up and down before the front
door, and their man-servant, William, informed them that it
belonged to the clergyman.

As they advanced to the verandah, Captain Carbonel and
his visitor came out to meet them, and Mr. Ashley Selby was
introduced. He looked more like a sportsman than a clergyman, except for his black coat; he had a happy, healthy, sunburnt face, top boots, and a riding-whip in his hand, and
informed Mrs. Carbonel that his father and mother would
have the honour of calling on her in a day or two. They had
an impression that he had come to reconnoitre and decide
whether they were farmers or gentry.

"We have been trying to make acquaintance with some of
your flock," said Mary.

"The last thing I would advise you to do," he answered;
"there are not a worse lot anywhere. Desperate poachers! Not a
head of game safe from them."

"Perhaps they may be improved."

He shrugged his shoulders. "See what my father has to say
of them."

"Is there much distress?"

"There ought not to be, for old Dr. Fogram and my father
send down a handsome sum for blankets and coals every
Christmas, and Uphill takes care to get its share!" He laughed.
"No sinecure distributing!"

"We have not been to see the school yet."

"A decrepit old crone, poor old body! She will soon have to
give in. She can't even keep the children from pulling off her

spectacles."

"And Sunday School?"

"Well, my father doesn't approve of cramming the poor children. I believe the Methodists have something of the kind at Downhill; but there is no one to attend to one here, and the place is quite free of dissent."

"Cause and effect?" said Captain Carbonel, drily.

"Would you object if we tried to teach the poor children something?" asked Mrs. Carbonel, cautiously.

"Oh no, not at all. All the good ladies are taking it up, I believe. Mrs. Grantley, of Poppleby, is great at it, and I see no harm in it; but you'll have to reckon with my father. He says there will soon be no ploughmen, and my mother says there will be no more cooks or housemaids. You'd better write to old Fogram, he'll back you up."

Mary had it on her lips to ask him about Widow Mole, but he had turned to Edmund to discuss the hunting and the shooting of the neighbourhood. They discovered, partly at this time, and partly from other visitors, that he was the younger son of the squire of Downhill, who had been made to take Holy Orders without any special fitness for it, because there was a living likely soon to be ready for him, and in the meantime he was living at home, an amiable, harmless young man, but bred up so as to have no idea of the duties of his vocation, and sharing freely in the sports of his family, acting as if he believed, like his father, that they were the most important obligations of man; and accepting the general household belief that only the Methodistical could wish for more religious practice.

Be it understood that all this happened in the earlier years of the century, and would be impossible under the revival of the Church that has since taken place. No one now can hold more than one piece of preferment at a time, so that parishes cannot be left unprovided. Nor could Ashley Selby be ordained without a preparation and examination which would have given him a true idea of what he undertook, or would have prevented his ordination. This, however, was at a time when the work of the church had grown very slack, and when a better spirit was beginning to revive. The father of Mary and Dora had been a zealous and earnest man, and both they and Edmund had really serious ideas of duty and of the means of carrying them out. In London they had heard sermons which had widened and deepened their views, but they had done no work, as the relation with whom they lived thought it impossible and improper for young ladies there. Thus they were exceedingly desirous of doing what they could to help the place where their lot was cast, and they set forth to reconnoitre. First, they found their way to the school, which stood on the border of the village green, a picturesque thatched cottage, with a honeysuckle and two tall poplars outside. But strange sounds guided them on their way, and the first thing they saw was a stout boy of four or five years old in petticoats bellowing loudly outside, and trying to climb the wicket gate which was firmly secured by a rusty chain. Mary tried to undo the gate, speaking meanwhile to the urchin, but he rushed away headlong back into the school, and they heard him howling, "They bees a-coming!"

A big girl in a checkered pinafore came out and made a curtsey, assisting to undo the chain.

"What has he been doing?" asked Dora.

"He be a mortial bad boy!" answered the girl. "He've been getting at Dame Verdon's sugar."

"And what is your name?" asked Mrs. Carbonel.

"Lizzie Verdon, ma'am. I helps Grannie."

Grannie did seem in need of help. There she sat in a big wooden chair by the fire, the very picture of an old dame, with a black bonnet, high-crowned and crescent shaped in front, with a white muslin cap below, a buff handkerchief crossed over her shoulders, a dark short-sleeved gown, long mittens covering her arms, and a checkered apron; a regular orthodox birch-rod by her side, and a black cat at her feet. But her head was shaking with palsy, and she hardly seemed to understand what Lizzie screamed into her ear that, "Here was the ladies."

But the door which they had shut in the face of their spaniel was thrust open. Up went the cat's back, bristle went her tail, her eyes shot sparks, and she bounded to the top of her mistress's chair. Dandy barked defiance, all the children shouted or screamed and danced about, and the old woman gasped and shook more. Lizzie alone was almost equal to the occasion. She flew at the cat who was standing on tiptoe on the tall back of the chair, with huge tail and eyes like green lamps, swearing, hissing, and spitting, and, regardless of scratches, caught him up by the scruff of his neck and disposed of him behind the staircase door; while Dora at the same moment secured Dandy by the collar, and rushing out, put him over the garden gate and shut both that and the door. Mary, afraid that the old lady was going to have a fit, went up to her with soothing apologies, but the unwonted sight seemed to confuse her the more, and she began crying. Lizzie, however, came to the rescue. She evidently had all her wits about her. First she called out: "Order, children. Don't you see the ladies? Sit down, Jem Hewlett, or I'll after you with the stick!" Then, as the children ranged themselves, she stamped at some to enforce her orders, shook the rod at others, and set up the smallest like so many ninepins, handling them by the shoulder on one small bench, interspersing the work with consolations to granny and explanations to the ladies, who were about to defer their visit.

"Granny, now never you mind. Tip is all right upstairs. Benny, you bad boy, I'll be at you. Don't go, please, lady. Bet, what be doin' to Jim? Never mind, granny! Susan Pucklechurch, you'll read to the lady, so pretty."

About five children, more tidily dressed than the others, had a whole and sound form to themselves near the fire and the mistress. The other two benches were propped, the one on two blocks of wood, the other on two sound and two infirm legs, and this was only balanced by a child at each end, so that when one got up the whole tumbled down or flew up, but the seat was very low, and the catastrophe generally produced mirth.

Susan Pucklechurch, granddaughter to the old bailiff and his Betty, was evidently the show scholar. "She be in her Testament, ma'am," explained Lizzie; and accordingly a terribly thumbed and dilapidated New Testament was put into the child's hand, from which she proceeded to bawl out, with long pauses between the words, and spelling the longest, a piece of the Sermon on the Mount, selected because there were no names in it. It was a painful performance to reverent ears, and as soon as practicable Mrs. Carbonel stopped it with "Good child!" and a penny, and asked what the others read. Those who were not "in the Testament" read the "Universal Spelling-book," provided at their own expense, but not in much better condition, and from this George Hewlett, son and heir to the carpenter, and a very different person from his cousin Jem, read the history of the defence of that city where each trade offered its own commodity for the defence, even to the cobbler, who proposed to lay in a stock of good l-e-a-t-h-e-r — lather!

These, and three little maidens who had picture spelling-books not going beyond monosyllables, were the aristocracy, and sat apart, shielded from the claws and teeth of their neigh-bours in consideration of paying fourpence, instead of two-pence, a week. The boy was supposed to write large letters on a slate, and the bigger girls did some needlework, and not badly — indeed, it was the best of their performances. The dame went on mumbling and shaking all the time, and it was quite evident that she was entirely past the work, and that Lizzie was the real mistress; indeed, Mrs. Carbonel was in-clined to give her credit for a certain talent for teaching and keeping order, when the sisters emerged from the close little oven of a place, hardly knowing whether to laugh or cry, but full of great designs.

Captain Carbonel, however, to their disappointment, ad-vised them to wait to set anything on foot till Dr. Fogram, the President of Saint Cyril's, came down in the summer holidays, when counsel could be taken with him, and there would be more knowledge of the subject. Dora did not like this at all. She was sure that the Son of Mist, as she was naughty enough to call the doctor, would only hamper them, and she was only half consoled by being told that there was no objection to her col-lecting a few of the children on Sunday and trying to teach them, and in the meantime acquaintance might be made with the mothers.

CHAPTER V.

At Home.

"Now I've gone through all the village, from end to end,
    save and except one more house;
But I haven't come to that, and I hope I never shall,
    and that's the village Poor House."

T. Hood.

Cottage visiting turned out to be a much chequered affair. One of the first places to which the sisters made their way was the Widow Mole's. They found it, rather beyond the church, down a lane, where it was hidden behind an overgrown thorn hedge, and they would scarcely have found it at all, if a three-year-old child had not been clattering an old bit of metal against the bar put across to prevent his exit. He was curly and clean, except with the day's surface dirt, but he only stared stolidly at the question whether Mrs. Mole lived there. A ten-year-old girl came out, and answered the question.

"Yes, mother do live here, but her be out at work."

"Is that your grandfather?" as they caught sight of a very old man on a chair by the door, in the sun.

"Yes, ma'am. Will you come in and see him?"

He was a very old man, with scanty white hair, but he was very clean, and neatly dressed in a white smock, mended all over, but beautifully worked over the breast and cuffs, and long leather buskins. He was very civil, too. He took off his old straw hat, and rose slowly by the help of his stout stick, though the first impulse of the visitors was to beg him not to move. He did not hear them, but answered their gesture.

"I be so crippled up with the rheumatics, you see, ma'am," and he put his knotted and contracted hand up to his ear.

Mrs. Carbonel shouted into his ear that she was sorry for him. She supposed his daughter was out at work.

"Yes, ma'am, with Farmer Goodenough — a charing today it is."

"Washing," screamed the little girl.

"She was off at five o'clock this morning," he went on. "She do work hard, my daughter Bess, and she's a good one to me, and so is little Liz here. Thank the Lord for them."

"And her husband is dead?"

"Yes, ma'am. Fell off a haystack three years ago, and never spoke no more. We have always kept off the parish, ma'am. This bit of a cottage was my poor wife's, and she do want to leave it to the boy; but she be but frail, poor maid, and if she gave in, there'd be nothing for it but to give up the place and go to the workhouse; and there's such a lot there as I could not go and die among."

He spoke it to the sympathising faces, not as one begging, and they found out that all was as he said. He had seen better days, and held his head above the parish pay, and so had his son-in-law but the early death of poor Mole, and the old man's crippled state, had thrown the whole maintenance of the family on the poor young widow, who was really working herself to death, while, repairs being impossible, the cottage was almost falling down.

"Oh, what a place, and what a dear old man!" cried the ladies, as they went out. "Well, we can do something here. I'll come and read to him every week," exclaimed Dora.

"And I will knit him a warm jacket," said Mary, "and surely Edmund could help them to prop up that wretched cottage."

"What a struggle their lives must have been, and so patient and good! Where are we going now?"

"I believe that is the workhouse, behind the church," said Mary. "That rough-tiled roof."

"It has a bend in the middle, like a broken back. I must sketch it," said Dora.

"Why, there's Edmund, getting over the churchyard stile."

"Ay, he can't keep long away from you, Madam Mary."

"Were you going to the workhouse?" said Captain Carbonel, coming up, and offering an arm to each lady, as was the fashion in those days.

"We thought of it. All the poorest people are there, of

course."

"And the worst," said the captain. "No, I will not have you go there. It is not fit for you."

For besides that he was very particular about his ladies, and had no notion of letting them go to all the varieties of evil where they could hope to do good, like the ladies of our days, the workhouse was an utterly different place from the strictly disciplined union houses of the present Poor Law. Each parish had its own, and that of Uphill had no master, no order, but was the refuge of all the disorderly, disreputable people, who could not get houses, or pay their rent, who lived in any kind of fashion, on parish pay and what they could get, and were under no restraint.

While the captain was explaining to them what he had heard from Farmer Goodenough, a sudden noise of shouting and laughing, with volleys of evil words, was heard near the "Fox and Hounds."

"What is that?" asked Dora, of a tidy young woman coming her way.

"That's only the chaps at old Sam," she answered, as if it was an ordinary sound. And on them exclaiming, she explained. "Samson Sanderson, that's his name, sir. He be what they calls non-compos, and the young fellows at the 'Fox and Hounds' they have their fun out of he. They do bait he shameful."

Violent shouts of foul words and riotous laughter could be distinguished so plainly, that Captain Carbonel hastily thrust his wife and sister into the nearest cottage, and marched into the group of rough men and boys, who stood holloaing rude jokes, and laughing at the furious oaths and abuse in intermittent gasps with which they were received.

"For shame!" his indignant voice broke in. "Are you not ashamed, unmanly fellows, to treat a poor weak lad in this way?"

There was a moment's silence. Then a great hulking drover called out, "Bless you, sir, he likes it."

"The more shame for you," exclaimed the captain, "to bait a poor innocent lad with horrid blasphemy and profanity. I tell you every one of you ought to be fined!"

The men began to sneak away from the indignant soldier. The poor idiot burst out crying and howling, and the ostler came forward, pulling his forelock, and saying, "You'll not be hard on 'em, sir. 'Tis all sport. There, Sammy, don't be afeared. Gentleman means you no harm."

Captain Carbonel held out some coppers, saying, "There, my poor lad, there's something for you. Only don't let me hear bad words again."

Sam muttered something, and pulled his ragged hat forward as he shambled off into some back settlements of the public-house, while the ostler went on —

"'Tis just their game, sir! None of 'em would hurt poor Sam! They'd treat him the next minute, sir. All in sport."

"Strange sport," said the captain, "to teach a poor helpless lad, who ought to be as innocent as a babe, that abominable blasphemy."

"He don't mean nought, sir! All's one to he!"

"All the worse in those who do know better, I tell you; and you may tell your master that, if this goes on, I shall certainly speak to the magistrates."

There was no need to tell the landlord, Mr. Oldfellow. The captain was plainly enough to be heard through the window of the bar. The drovers had no notion that their amusement was sinful, for "it didn't hurt no one," and, in fact, "getting a rise" out of Softy Sam was one of the great attractions of the "Fox and Hounds," so that Mr. Oldfellow was of the same mind as Dan Hewlett, who declared that "they Gobblealls was plaguey toads of Methodys, and wasn't to think to bully them about like his soldiers."

They had another drink all round to recover from their fright, when they treated Softy Sam, but took care not to excite him to be noisy, while the captain might be within earshot.

The two ladies had meanwhile taken refuge in what proved to be no other than Mrs. Daniel Hewlett's house, a better one, and less scantily provided with furniture, than the widow Mole's, but much less clean and neat. The door stood open, and there was a tub full of soap-suds within. The captain gave a low whistle to intimate his presence, and stood at the entrance. Unwashed dinner things were on a round table, a dresser in confusion against the wall, on another Moore's Almanack for some years past, full of frightful catastrophes, mixed with little, French, highly-coloured pictures of the Blessed Virgin.

His wife and her sister were seated, the one on a whole straw chair, the other on a rickety one, conversing with a very neat, pale, and pleasant-looking invalid young woman, evidently little able to rise from her wooden armchair. Molly Hewlett, in a coarse apron, and a cap far back amid the rusty black tangles of her hair, her arms just out of the wash-tub, was in the midst of a voluble discourse, into which the ladies would not break.

"You see, ma'am, she was in a right good situation, but she was always unlucky, and she had the misfortune to fall down the attic stairs with the baby in her arms."

"The baby was not hurt," put in the invalid.

"Not it, the little toad, but 'twas saving he as ricked her back somehow, and made her a cripple for life, as you see, ma'am; and she was six months in the hospital, till the doctor, he say as how he couldn't do nothing more for her, so Hewlett and me we took her in, as she is my own sister, you see, and we couldn't let her go to the workhouse, but she do want a little broth or a few extrys now and then, ma'am, more than we poor folks can give her."

"My mistress is very good, and gives me a little pension," put in the invalid, while her sister looked daggers at her, and Mrs. Carbonel, in obedience to her husband's signal, took a hasty leave.

"There now! That's the way of you, Judith," cried Molly Hewlett, banging the door behind them. "What should you go for to tell the ladies of that pitiful pay of yours but to spile all chance of their helping us, nasty, mean skin-flints as they be!"

"I couldn't go for to deceive them," humbly replied Judith, meek, but cowering under the coming storm.

"Who asked you to deceive? Only to hold your tongue for your own good, and mine and my poor children's, that you just live upon. As if your trumpery pay was worth your board and all the trouble I has with you night and day, but you must come in and hinder these new folk from coming down liberal with your Methody ways and your pride! That's it, your pride, ma'am. Oh, I'm an unhappy woman, between you and Dan! I am!"

Molly sank into a chair, put her apron over her face and cried, rocking herself to and fro, while Judith, with tears in her eyes, tried gentle consolations all in vain, till Molly remembered her washing, and rose up, moaning and lamenting.

Meantime Mrs. Carbonel and her sister were exclaiming in pity that this was a dear good girl, though Edmund shook his head over her surroundings.

"I wonder how to make her more comfortable," said Dora. "She seemed so much pleased when I promised to bring her something to read."

"I am afraid those Hewletts prey on her," said Mary.

"And patronising her will prove a complicated affair!" said the captain.

He wanted them to come home at once, but on the way they met Nanny Barton, who began, with low curtsies, a lamentable story about her girls having no clothes, and she would certainly have extracted a shilling from Miss Carbonel if the captain had not been there.

"Never accept stories told on the spur of the moment," he said.

Then Betsy Seddon and Tirzah Todd came along together, bending under heavy loads of broken branches for their fires. Tirzah smiled as usual, and showed her pretty teeth, but the captain looked after her, and said, "They have been tearing Mr. Selby's woods to pieces."

"What can they do for firewood?" said his wife.

"Let us look out the rules of your father's coal store and shoe club," he said.

CHAPTER VI.

The Neighbourhood.

"Through slush and squad,
When roads was bad,
But hallus stop at the Vine and Hop."

Tennyson.

Through all Pucklechurch's objections and evident contempt for his fancies, and those of young madam, Captain Carbonel insisted on the clearance of the yard. He could not agree with the old man, who made free to tell him that, "Such as that there muck-heap was just a bucket to a farmer's wife, if she was to be called a farmer's wife — was that it."

With some reflection, Captain Carbonel decided that a bucket might mean a bouquet, and answered, "Maybe she might have too much of a good thing. When I went down to Farmer Bell's the other day, they had a famous heap, and I was struck with the sickly look of his wife and daughters."

"His missus were always a poor, nesh 'ooman," returned Pucklechurch.

"And I don't mean mine to be like her if I can help it," said the captain.

But he did not reckon on the arrival of a prancing pair of horses, with a smart open carriage, containing two ladies and a gentleman, in the most odorous part of the proceedings, when he was obliged to clear the way from a half-loaded waggon to make room for them, and, what was quite as inconvenient, to hurry up the back stairs to his dressing-room to take off his long gaiters, Blucher boots (as half high ones were then called) and old shooting coat, and make himself presentable.

In fact, when he came into the room, Dora was amused at the perceptible look of surprised approval of the fine tall soldierly figure, as he advanced to meet Mr. and Mrs. Selby and their daughter, the nearest neighbours, who were, of course, in the regular course of instruction of the newcomers in the worthlessness and ingratitude of Uphill and the impossibility of doing anything for the good of the place.

Mary was very glad that he interrupted the subject by saying merrily, "You caught me in the midst of my Augean stable. I hope next time you are kind enough to visit us that the yard may be in a more respectable condition."

Mr. Selby observed that it was unpardonable not to have done the work beforehand, and the captain answered, "On the contrary, it was reserved as a fragrant bucket, or bouquet for a farmer's wife."

Whereat the visitors looked shocked, and Mary made haste to observe: "But we do hope to make a better road to the house through the fields."

"There is a great deal to be done first," said Dora, who thought the observation rather weak.

Nothing else that was interesting took place on this occasion. Mr. Selby asked the captain whether he hunted, and gave him some information on the sport of all kinds in the neighbourhood. Miss Selby asked Dora if she liked archery, music, and drawing. Mrs. Selby wanted to recommend a housemaid, and advised Mrs. Carbonel against ever taking a servant from the neighbourhood. And then they all turned to talk of the evil doings of the parish thieves, poachers, idlers, drunkards, and to warn the Carbonels once more against hoping to improve them. The horses could be heard pawing and jingling outside, and, as the ladies rose to take leave, Captain Carbonel begged leave to hurry out and clear the coast. And it was well that he did so, for he had to turn back a whole procession of cows coming in to be milked, and sundry pigs behind them.

The farm court was finished, and never was so bad again, the animals being kept from spending their day there, except the poultry, in which Mary took great delight. Soon came more visitors, and it became a joke to the husband and sister that she always held out hopes of "the future drive" when they arrived, bumped or mired by the long lane. "Mary's Approach," as Edmund called it, had to be deferred till more needful work was done. The guests whom they best liked, Mr. and Mrs.

Grantley, the clergyman and his wife from the little town of Poppleby, gave an excellent and hopeful account of their rector, Dr. Fogram, who was, they said, a really good man, and very liberal.

Mrs. Grantley was interested in schools and poor people, as it was easy to discover, and Mary and Dora were soon talking eagerly to her, and hearing what was done at Poppleby; but there were gentry and prosperous tradespeople there, who could be made available as subscribers or teachers; so that their situation was much more hopeful than that of the Carbonels, who had not the authority of the clergyman.

Poppleby was a much larger place than Downhill, on the post road to London. The mail-coach went through it, and thence post-horses were hired, and chaises, from the George Inn. The Carbonels possessed a phaeton, and a horse which could be used for driving or riding, and thus Captain Carbonel took the two ladies to return the various calls that had been made upon them. They found the Selbys not at home, but were warmly welcomed by the Grantleys, and spent the whole afternoon with them, and, at Dora's earnest request, were taken to see the schools. So different was the taste and feeling of those days that, though Poppleby Church was a very fine old one — in grand architecture, such as in these days is considered one of the glories of the country — no one thought of going to look at it, and the effect of Mr. Grantley's excellent sermons had been the putting up of a new gallery right across the chancel arch.

It had a fine tower and steeple, and this Dora thought of as a delightful subject for a sketch from the Parsonage garden. She made great friends with Lucy Grantley, the eldest daughter, over their tastes in drawing, as well as in the Waverley novels and in poetry, and was invited to spend a long day at Poppleby and take a portrait of the steeple.

After the calls had been made and returned began the dinner-parties. Elmour Priory was so near Greenhow that it would have been easy to walk there across the fields, or to drive in the phaeton, especially as the hours were much earlier, and six or half-past was held to be a late dinner hour, but this would have been contrary to etiquette, especially the first time, with people who evidently thought much of "style," and the Carbonels were not superior to such considerations, which were — or were supposed to be — of more importance in those days. So a chaise was ordered, and they went in state, and had a long, dull evening, chiefly enlivened by the Miss Selbys and Dora playing on the piano.

As they were going home, all round by the road, when they were near the top of the hill, before they came to the "Fox and Hounds," the postilion first shouted and then came to a sudden stop. The captain, putting his head out at the window, saw by the faint light of a young moon, going down in the remains of sunset, that he was jumping off his horse, growling and swearing, but under his breath, when the captain sprang out. A woman was lying across the road, and had barely escaped being run over. Mary and Dora were both out in a moment.

"Poor thing, poor thing! Is it a fit? She is quite insensible."

"A fit of a certain kind," said the captain, who was dragging her into the hedge, while the post-boy held the horses. "Go back, Mary, Dora!"

"It is Nanny Barton!" said Dora in horror.

Mary took down one of the carriage lamps and held it to the face. "Yes, it is!" said she. "Can't we take her home, or do anything?"

"No, no; nonsense!" said Edmund. "Don't come near, don't touch her. Don't you see, she is simply dead drunk."

"But we can't leave her here."

"The best thing to do! Yes, it is; but we will stop at the 'Fox and Hounds,' if that will satisfy you, and send some one out to see after her."

They were obliged to be satisfied, for the tones were authoritative, and they had to accept his assurance that the woman was in no state for them to meddle with. She would come to no harm, he said, when he had put her on the bank, and it was only to pacify them that he caused the postilion to stop at the public-house, whence roaring, singing, and shouts proceeded. The landlord came out, supposing it was some new arrival, and when Captain Carbonel jumped out, and, speaking severely, desired that some one would go to look after the woman, who was lying in the road, and whom the horses had almost run over, he answered as if he had been doing the most natural and correct thing in the world.

"Yes, sir; I had just sent her home. They had been treating of her, and she had had a drop too much. She wasn't in a proper state."

"Proper state! No! I should think not! It is a regular shame and disgrace that you should encourage such goings on! Where's the woman's husband? Has no one got the humanity to come and take her home?"

Oldfellow called gruffly to some of the troop, who came reeling out to the door, and told them it was time to be off, and that some one, "You Tirzah had best see to that there Barton 'oman."

Captain Carbonel wished to keep his ladies from the sight, but they were watching eagerly, and could not help seeing that it was Tirzah Todd, more gipsy-looking than ever, who came out. Not, however, walking as if intoxicated, and quite able to comprehend Captain Carbonel's brief explanation where to find her companion.

"Ah, poor Nanny!" she said cheerfully. "She's got no head! A drop is too much for her."

The chaise door was shut, and they went on, Dora and Mary shocked infinitely, and hardly able to speak of what they had seen.

And they did not feel any happier when the next day, as Mary was feeding the chickens, Nanny came up to her curtseying and civil.

"Please, ma'am, I'm much obliged to you for seeing to me last night. I just went in to see if my husband was there, as was gone to Poppleby with some sheep, and they treated me, ma'am. And that there Tirzah and Bet Bracken, they was a-singing songs, as it was a shame to hear, so I ups and rebukes them, and she flies at me like a catamount, ma'am; and then Mr. Oldfellow, he puts me out, ma'am, as was doing no harms as innocent as a lamb."

"Well," said Mrs. Carbonel, "it was no place for any woman

to be in, and we were grieved, I cannot tell you how much, that you should be there. You had better take care; you know drunkenness is a really wicked sin in God's sight."

"Only a little overtaken — went to see for my husband," muttered Nanny. "I didn't take nigh so much as that there Tirzah Todd, that is there with Bet Bracken every night of her life, to sing — "

"Never mind other people. Their doing wrong doesn't make you right."

"Only a drop," argued Nanny. "And that there Tirzah and Bet — "

Mary was resolved against hearing any more against Tirzah and Bet, and actually shut herself into the granary till Nanny was gone. And there she sat down on a sack of peas and fairly cried at the thought of the sin and ignorant unconsciousness of evil all round her. And then she prayed a little prayer for help and wisdom for these poor people and themselves. Then she felt cheered up and hopeful.

CHAPTER VII.

Sunday School.

"She hastens to the Sunday School."
Jane Taylor.

Captain Carbonel had written to the President of Saint Cyril's, and at once obtained his willing consent to the ladies attempting to form a little Sunday School. Dr. Fogram said that he should come down himself on July 21, and should be very glad to take counsel with the Carbonels on the state of Uphill. He would be glad to assist if any outlay were needed.

The sisters were in high spirits. The only place they could find for the purpose was the wash-house and laundry. Once in five weeks two women, in high white muslin caps and checked aprons, of whom Betsy Seddon was one, Betty Pucklechurch the other, came to assist the maids in getting up the family linen — a tremendous piece of work. A tub was set on the Saturday, with ashes placed in a canvas bag on a frame above; water was poured on it, and ran through, so as to be fitted for the operations which began at five o'clock in the morning, and absorbed all the women of the establishment, and even old Pucklechurch, who was called on to turn the mangle.

Except during this formidable week, the wash-house and laundry were empty, and hither were invited the children. About twenty, of all ages, came — the boys in smocks, the girls in print frocks and pinafores, one in her mother's black bonnet, others in coarse straw or sun-bonnets. All had shoes of some sort, but few had stockings, though the long frocks concealed the deficiencies, and some wore stocking-legs without feet.

They made very low bows, or pulled their forelocks, most grinned and looked sheepish, and a very little one began to cry. It did not seem very promising, but Mary and Dora began by asking all their names, and saying they hoped to be better friends. They, for the most part, knew nothing, with the exception of George Hewlett's two eldest, Bessie Mole's girls, and one sharp boy of Dan Hewlett's, also the Pucklechurch grand-children; but even these had very dim notions, and nobody but the Hewletts could tell a word of the Catechism.

To teach them the small commencement of doctrine comprised in the earliest pages of "First Truths" was all that could be attempted, as well as telling them a Bible story, to which the few intelligent ones listened with pleasure, and Johnnie Hewlett showed that he had already heard it — "from aunt," he said. He was a sickly, quiet-looking boy, very different from his younger brother, Jem, who had organised a revolt among the general multitude before long. None of these had enough civilisation to listen or be attentive for five minutes together, and when Mrs. Carbonel looked round on hearing a howl, there was a pitched battle going on between Jem and Lizzie Seddon over her little sister, who had been bribed into coming with a lump of gingerbread, which the boy was abstracting. He had been worked up enough even to lose his awe of the ladies, and to kick and struggle when Dora, somewhat imprudently, tried to turn him out.

The disturbance was so great that the sisters were obliged to dismiss their pupils at least a quarter of an hour sooner than they had intended, and without having tried to teach the short daily prayers that had been part of the programme.

Somewhat crestfallen they sped back to the house.

"Did you ever see such a set of little savages?" cried Dora.

"Come, there was a very fair proportion of hopeful ones," was the reply.

These hopeful ones made one class under Dora, while Mary, who had more patience and experience, undertook the others, who, when once wakened, proved very eager and interested, in a degree new to those who are not the first lights in gross darkness. Johnnie Hewlett was the brightest among the children, for though his weekdays were occupied in what his mother called "keeping a few birds," or, more technically, "bird-starving," he spent most of his spare time beside his sick aunt, and had not only been taught by her to read, but to think, and to say his prayers.

As Dora gradually learnt, both Mary Hewlett and Judith

Grey had been children of a little "smock-frock" farmer, and had not been entirely without breeding; but Molly had been the eldest, and had looked after the babies, and done much of the work of the farm, till she plunged into an early and most foolish marriage with the ne'er-do-well member of the old sawyer's family, and had been going deeper into the mire ever since.

Judith, a good deal younger, and always delicate, had gone to the dame school when Mrs. Verdon was rather less inefficient, and at ten years old had been taken into service by an old retired servant, who needed her chiefly as a companion, and thence she had been passed on to a family where the ladies were very kind to the servants, and the children brought them their books and their information of all kinds, so that she had much cultivation, religious and otherwise.

When her accident had sent her home to the only surviving member of her family, she hoped to be of use to her sister and the children; but, before long, she found it almost hopeless. Molly, indeed, was roughly kind to her, but Dan took no notice of her except to "borrow" her money, and any attempt to interfere with the management of the children was resented.

Johnnie, the eldest boy, was fond of his aunt, and soon became her best attendant when not out at the work that began at nine years old. He was willing that she should teach him, and when the ladies came to see her she was full of stories of what he had told her. She said no word of the rudeness of the girls or the tyranny of Jem, as she sat helpless by the fire. When all were out, these were pleasant peaceful visits to her, and she was grateful for the books Dora lent her, and the needlework Mrs. Carbonel gave her when she was well enough to do it. Molly was not unwilling that her sister should be "a fav'rite," as she called it, more especially as Jem was generally allowed to swallow any dainty brought by the ladies that was to his taste.

Old Master Redford, Widow Mole's father, was another cheerful spot in the village. He was a thoroughly good, devout person in a simple way, and most grateful for Dora's coming to read to him. Old Pucklechurch once, indeed, said, "What, ma'am, ye be never a-going to read to that there Thomas Redford! Why, 'tis all one as singing Psalms to a dead horse."

In spite, however, of this hopeless augury, Dora's voice did reach his ears. He had made good use of his scanty opportunities, and had taught his family to be thoroughly conscientious. There was another daughter in service, who from time to time sent him a little help, but the transit of money was a difficulty in those days, and the relief could not often come. One morning Widow Mole fainted away in the hayfield, and hardly heard Farmer Goodenough abusing her fine-lady airs, though she trembled and shook so much when she tried to go on that she was forced to let Tirzah Todd lead her home, and the next morning she could not get up.

She had been in such plight before, and the shop trusted her, knowing that she always strove to pay off her debts, but the farmer rated her vehemently, declaring that she had been good for nothing since the ladies had been putting fancies and megrims in her head, and that he would not take her on again. Probably he did not mean to fulfil his threat, for, as far as her strength allowed, she was the best and most thorough worker of all his women, and he had no desire to have the whole family on the rates; but the ladies believed it, and came home furious with indignation, and even Captain Carbonel thought her justified in accepting the dismissal, and as soon as "kitchen physic" had a little restored her, she became washer-woman, weeding woman, and useful woman generally at Greenhow Farm.

Many a cup of tea and thick slice of bread-and-butter were carried out to her after breakfast, not to say three-cornered remnant of pie, or sandwich of cold meat at luncheon; and, though some was saved for "granfer and the children," still she began to look like another woman ere many weeks were over.

Betsy Seddon and Molly Hewlett were much displeased, and reproached her with having got the place by "hypercriting about."

Nanny Barton put on a white apron and brought out the big Bible when she saw the ladies getting over the stile. The first time Dora was much delighted; the second, Mrs. Carbonel managed to see that the Bible was open at one of the genealogies in the First Book of Chronicles, and spied besides the dirtiest of all skirts under the apron. After that she did not much heed when Nanny said she would come to church if her shoes were not so bad.

Tirzah Todd laughed and showed her white teeth and merry eyes so pleasantly that no one could help liking to talk with her, but alas! old Pucklechurch took care to let them know that she could be just as merry in a different way at the "Fox and Hounds."

CHAPTER VIII.

Mary's Approach.

"The chaise was stayed,
But yet was not allowed
To drive up to the door, lest all
Should say that she was proud."

Cowper.

Dr. Fogram was true to his word, and made his appearance at the Long Vacation. The Carbonels, to whom little eager Sophia had been added a day or two previously, first saw him at Downhill Church, where he made a most dignified appearance, in a very full surplice, with his Doctor of Divinity's red hood over it. The clerk, small, grey-haired, and consequential, bustled up to open the pulpit door for him, and he preached, in a fine, sonorous voice, a very learned sermon, that might have been meant for his undergraduates at Oxford.

It was the day for afternoon service at Uphill, so the sisters had to hurry away to eat their luncheon in haste, and then to introduce Sophy to the Sunday School, where she was to teach a class of small ones, a matter of amazing importance and ecstasy.

She was a damsel of thirteen, in a white frock and cape, a pink sash, pink kerchief round her neck, pink satin ribbons tying down her broad Leghorn hat over her ears, in what was called gipsy fashion. She had rosy cheeks, blue, good-natured eyes, and shining, light-brown curls all round her head. Her appearance in the school was quite as memorable to the children as Dr. Fogram's could be to their elders, and the little ones were so engaged in looking at her that they quite forgot to be naughty, except that Billy Mole, in curiosity to know what anything so glossy and shining could be, pinched the end of her sash, and left the grimy mark of his little hot hands on it, which caused Maitland the maid, who had charge of her toilette, to declare that such things always came of going among "they nasty, dirty little brats."

Dr. Fogram rode over on a plump, shining, black horse, followed by a well-equipped groom. He dismounted, and gave his horse to the man when he overtook the Carbonel party on the way up the hill.

"Captain Carbonel, I believe," said he, touching his hat, almost a shovel. "Will you do me the honour to introduce me to the ladies," and to them he uncovered with the grand formal politeness which even then was becoming rather old-fashioned and which they returned with curtsies, Sophia's, being fresh from the dancing-master, the most perfect of all.

"I understand," said he, "that I am greatly indebted to you for pains taken with this unfortunate parish."

"We have been trying to do what we could," said Mrs. Carbonel, to whom this was chiefly addressed.

"It is a great kindness," he replied, "and I hope the people may show themselves sensible of your exertions, but hitherto all endeavours for their benefit have been thrown away."

Dora could not help wondering what the exertions were!

After the service he joined the family again, and said that he thought the appearance of the poor — and especially of the children — and their behaviour much improved, and he had no doubt it was owing to the gentle and beneficent influence of the ladies, to whom he bowed.

In fact, the children had been much engaged in staring, though whether he or Sophy were the prime attraction, might be doubtful. At any rate, Master Pucklechurch's rod had only once descended. Moreover, two neat sun-bonnets of lilac print adorned two heads, and the frocks looked as if they were sometimes washed.

Captain Carbonel said he hoped to have some conversation with the President about the parish; and he responded that he hoped to do himself the honour of calling the next day. After which he mounted his horse and rode off.

The three sisters waited and watched as if their whole fate depended on the morning's conference but nothing was seen of the President till after luncheon, when he rode up, attended by his groom as before. To their great disappointment, he would talk of nothing but the beauty of the country, and of the voices of Lablache and Sonntag, or the like, which he evidently considered the proper subjects for ladies; and it was not till he had spent the quarter of an hour, fit for a visit of ceremony, on these topics that he asked Captain Carbonel to allow him a little conversation with him.

They shut themselves into the captain's little 'den,' which was something between a gun-room and a library, with the rectory books going round two sides of the room, Edmund's sword, pistols, and spurs hanging over the mantelpiece, and his guns, shot-belts, powder-horn, and fishing-rods on hooks on the wall. No noise was heard for more than an hour, during which Dora fumed, Mary cut off the dead roses, and Sophia was withheld from peeping.

At last they came out — the horses had been brought to the door — the President bowed to the ladies, mounted, and rode off, while Edmund came across the lawn; and they all clustered round him.

"Well," said he, "we have fared better than we expected. Dr. Fogram has long been regretting the state of the parish."

"Why did he do nothing?" broke in Dora.

"I suppose he has much on his hands; and, I am afraid, my poor old uncle was a hindrance, for he really seemed like a man who had got rid of an incubus when he found that we were willing to do what we could. Then it seems that he was disappointed in Ashley Selby. He thought that, being an inhabitant of the place, the young man would be interested in the people, and make his sisters useful."

"They!" exclaimed Dora. "They are such fine ladies, who think about nothing but Almack's, are afraid of the dirt, and of catching all sorts of disorders at the cottages."

"I can hardly get Dora to be moderately civil to them," said Mary.

"Yes," said Edmund, "parental influence has been strong. The mother fears for health, the father for his game, and the children have grown up to think poachers and their families almost beyond the pale of humanity. It has been too much for this young man, who simply acquiesced in the way in which he was bred. However, this will come to an end, for the present holder of the family living has had a paralytic stroke, and wants him to come and assist. I fully believe that he may do much better away from home habits, especially under a good incumbent."

"And what is to happen to us?" inquired Mary.

"Dr. Fogram says that he will send us one of the Fellows of his college — a young man full of zeal, who is eager for parochial work, and has been taking duty at a parish some miles from Oxford. He thinks we shall be satisfied with the change."

"As if we were the people to be satisfied," cried Dora. "Just confess, Edmund, that the old gentleman did not think the place worth attending to till educated gentlefolk came to live in it."

"Say, rather, that he really did not know the deficiencies," said the captain, "till they were brought before him."

"Then he ought," muttered Dora.

"Judge not," whispered Mary, who was a reverent person.

"And the school?" resumed Dora. "Was he aware of any deficiency there?"

"He was very glad to hear that you had begun keeping school, and will contribute to a better arrangement for the weekday school, assist in pensioning off Dame Verdon, if needful, and in obtaining a better person."

Dora and Sophy each gave a little caper, and squeezed one another's hands.

"He is quite disposed to be liberal," continued Edmund; "and I am sure we shall find him no impediment."

"I don't think the school is going on now," said Mary. "Lizzie Verdon came for some broth, and said Granny was bad in bed. I asked whether she had had the doctor, and she stared and said no, but Dame Spurrell had got her some 'yarbs.'"

For in those days the union doctor was not an institution. Large tracts of country would contract with some apothecary to attend their sick; but he was generally a busy man, with his hands full of paying patients, and there was nobody to keep him up to his work among the poor, if he could have done it, which he really could not. The poor themselves knew that it was in vain to apply to him, or if he came once in a serious case, to expect any attention; and they preferred to depend on the woman clever in "yarbs," on the white witch, or, in favoured villages, on the lady bountiful or the clergyman and his wife; and in simple cases these latter were quite efficient, keeping a family medicine-chest and a book on household medicine.

Mrs. Carbonel had rooted out her mother's book, replenished her chest, and had cured two or three children who had been eating unripe apples, and greatly benefited Mole with infusions of Jesuit's bark in a large jug, the same thing as quinine, only more cumbrously and domestically prepared. But most of the Uphill people had the surest confidence in Dame Spurrell and her remedies, some of which were very curious; for Mrs. Carbonel found a child who had fits wearing, in a bag, a pinch of black hair from the cross on the back of a jackass; and once, when she objected to a dirty mark on the throat of Susan Pucklechurch, she was told it was left by a rasher of bacon put on to cure a sore throat.

The symptoms were sometimes curious as she now found when she went to inquire after Dame Verdon, who, Lizzie informed her, had her heart hanging by only one string, and when that gave way, she would not be here.

For the present, however, she was in bed, under a quilt made of coloured cloth scraps; but however it might be with her heart-strings, she did not seem likely to get up again. It was hay time, and it appeared that no one did come to school in hay and harvest seasons, so that there was time to consider what could be done. Dr. Fogram was invited to dinner to hold consultation with the ladies, whom the captain would not leave to any conclusion as to the schools.

There were no such things as trained masters and mistresses in those days; the National Society had only been in existence eleven years, and Government had not taken up the matter at all. Educated and religious people had, however, come to the conclusion that it would be well to help all the village children to know their faith and duty, and to read their Bibles; and the good work of Mrs. Hannah More and Mrs. Trimmer were examples that had begun to be followed, now that the one was in extreme old age, and the other in her grave. The Carbonel family had been bred up to such work, and all of them knew a good deal more about it than the President, whose studies had been chiefly in Greek plays, and whose tasks had been dealing with young men and the college estates. His conscience as a clergyman was a good deal stirred by the condition of his parish, and he was really thankful to those who would take up the matter, as well as ready to assist with his purse.

So it was settled that Mrs. Carbonel should write about a widow at her old home, who had once been a servant in the family. She was known to be a good religious person, who could read, and write, and cast accounts quite well enough for any possibly advanced scholars, as well as being a beautiful needlewoman. An old friend went to see her, explain the situation to her, and ascertain if she were willing to undertake the school for twenty pounds a year, and what the children could pay.

A cottage belonging to Captain Carbonel might have a room added to it to receive the scholars, by the end of harvest, by which time they might be got together, and Mrs. Verdon was to be induced to resign by a pension of half-a-crown a week, a sum then supposed to be ample, and which, indeed, was so for her wants, which were much less than in these days. Captain Carbonel looked over the cottage, and worked out an estimate of the cost with old Hewlett, whose notions of paper work were of the kind shown in his Midsummer bill.

	shillings	pence
1 ooden barrer a oodnt soot	9	6
1 ooden barrer a ood soot	9	6

The result of the calculations, conjectural and otherwise, was this.

"Mary, look here. This is an expensive year, and if we do the thing this year, we must put off making the drive through the fields — your approach, madam."

Mary came and looked at his figures. "How will it be after harvest?" she said.

"Harvest is an inappreciable quantity, especially to novices," he said. "If you believe Farmer Goodenough, the finest weather will not save me from finding myself out of pocket."

"Farmer Goodenough is an old croaker, after his kind," said Mary.

"It won't do to reckon thereupon. I must be secure of capital enough to fall back upon. Think it over well, Mary, and answer me tomorrow; and you had better say nothing to your sisters till your own mind is made up. I own that I should be very glad of the road. It would save us and old Major a good deal, to say nothing of our friends' bones."

"Do you mean that you wish it, Edmund?"

"I wish to leave it entirely to you."

Dora and Sophy had gone across the fields, a four miles' walk to Poppleby, and were to be brought home in the evening, and Mary was left to wander about the old road and the field-path, and meditate on the ruts and quagmires that would beset the way in the winter, and shut them up from visiting, perhaps even from church. Besides, there were appearances!

There was an old gentleman, a far-away connection of Edmund's, who had been in the navy, and now lived at Poppleby, and went about collecting all the chatter to be heard in one house, and retailing it all in another, and he thought himself licensed to tell Edmund and Mary everything personal. One thing was —

"My dear fellow, you should really put a check on your wife's Methodistical ways!"

"I didn't know she had any."

"I have been told, on good authority, that she has a meeting every Sunday in the wash-house."

Edmund laughed. "A dozen children for Sunday School, with the President's full consent."

"It won't do, Edmund. You'll find it won't do! Why, old Selby told me she was a pretty creature, only just like your good pious ladies, running into all the dirtiest cottages."

And to Mary it was, "Let me give you a hint, my dear Mrs. Carbonel. The Duchess saw you in Poppleby, and asked who you were, and she said she would like to visit you, if you did not live in such a hole."

"I don't think I want her," said Mary.

"Now, my dear, don't you be foolish! It would be so much to Edmund's advantage! He was in the same regiment with Lord Henry, and you might have the best society in the county, if only you would make your new drive! Why, even Lady Hartman says she can't take her horses again through that lane, or into the farm court. Miss Yates said it was quite disgusting."

Mary Carbonel might laugh. She did not care for her own dignity, but she did for Edmund's; and though she had been amused at Lady Hartman's four horses entangled in the narrow sweep, and did not quite believe old Captain Caiger, the lady herself had been very charming, and Mary did not like to cut her husband and sisters off from the pleasantest houses in the country.

But the words, "Love not the world," came up into her mind, and the battle ended by her saying to her husband —

"Don't let us have the approach this year, dear Edmund. I don't want it to be Mary's reproach."

"You are quite sure? In spite of Caiger?"

"Indeed I am; though I am afraid it is asking you to give up something."

"Not while I have my merry faces at home, Mary. And indeed, little woman, I am glad of your decision. It is right."

"I am so glad!"

CHAPTER IX.

The Screen.

"There is no honesty in such dealing."
— *Shakespeare.*

One day when Sophy had been trusted to go out alone to carry a few veal cutlets from luncheon to Judith, she found the door on the latch, but no one in the room downstairs, the chair empty, the fire out, and all more dreary than usual, only a voice from above called out, "Please come up."

Sophy, pleased with the adventure, mounted the dark and rickety stairs, and found herself in the open space above, cut off from the stairs by a screen, and containing a press-bed, where Judith lay, covered by an elaborate patchwork quilt. There was a tiny dressing-table under the narrow lattice window, and one chair, also a big trunk-box, with a waggon-shaped lid, such as servants used to have in those days, covered with paper, where big purple spots of paint concealed the old print of some story or newspaper. On the wall hung a few black profiles, and all was very fairly neat, whatever the room might be shut off by a wooden partition, whence came a peculiar sour smell.

"Oh, it is Miss Sophia!" exclaimed Judith. "I beg your pardon, ma'am, I thought it was Dame Spurrell, who said she would come and look in on me, or I would not have troubled you to come up."

"I am glad I did, Judith; I like to see where you live. Only, are you worse?"

"No, miss, only as my back is sometimes, and my sister and all the children are gone to the hiring fair, so it was not handy to get me up."

"And this is your room!" said Sophy, looking about her. "Isn't it very cold?"

"Johnnie heats me a brick to keep me warm at night; but my feet are always cold downstairs. It does not make much difference."

"Oh dear! And you have a screen, I see. Oh! Why, that is our drawing-room paper."

She sat transfixed at the recognition, while Judith observed, quite innocently, with a free conscience —

"Yes, miss, my brother-in-law brought it home, and told me it was just a scrap that was left over, and he was free to have, though I said I did wonder the lady did not want to keep it in case of an accident happening."

"Yes," said Sophy, "I don't think he had any business to have it, for all one division of the paper is put on upside down. The laburnums point up instead of hanging down, and I am sure Mary would have altered it if she could. It was beautiful French paper that Edmund brought home from Paris and laid up for the furnishing their house."

This, of course, Mrs. Carbonel and Dora would never have told poor Judith, but Sophy was young and unguarded, and apt to talk when she had better have held her tongue.

"I am sorry to hear it, miss, indeed I am. I am afraid one could not take it off the screen to put it back again where it did ought to be."

Sophy looked, but it was manifestly impossible. Spoiling the screen would not mend the wall of the drawing-room.

"Perhaps Molly might have another bit left," she said, only thinking of the triumph of carrying home the means of repairing the deficiency by her own unassisted sagacity.

"I will ask her, miss. I am sure I never thought Dan would go for to do such a thing," mourned Judith, though, even as she spoke, there came back on her recollections of times when she had tried to be blind and deaf. "But if Mrs. Carbonel would let me pay for it, miss, I should be easier in my mind. I have a shilling, though no doubt that is not the worth of it." And she began feeling for a little box under her pillow, never mentioning that she had already paid Dan a shilling for it.

"No, no; nonsense, Judith! Of course my sister would not take it for the world; but if any one could find another bit, just to patch up the part above the bookcase, it would be nice."

"I will do what in me lays, Miss Sophy," answered Judith.

So Sophy took her leave and trotted home, very proud of her discovery, which she communicated in an eager voice as the phaeton drew up at the front door.

"Oh, Edmund, I have found the rest of the drawing-room paper!"

"Hush! not so loud, my dear," said Dora, getting out of the back seat, and Edmund, being busy in telling the groom to attend to something in the harness, did not heed at first.

"Did you know, Dora?" asked Sophy, in a lower voice, being struck by something in her repressive manner.

"Yes; but I did not tell, because Edmund was so much vexed, and it was of no use now."

Dora really hoped no one had heard, as Mary was busy with her parcels, and she was too fond of Judith not to wish to shield her family; but it was too late. The captain came in with, "What's this about the drawing-room paper?"

Sophy was delighted to pour out the history of her discovery, and tell how it appeared on the screen that sheltered poor Judith Grey.

"Exactly as I supposed," said Captain Carbonel. "I always believed that fellow was a thief."

"But it is not poor Judith's fault," exclaimed the sisters, with one voice.

"She knew nothing about it. She wanted to pay the shilling for it," said Sophia.

The captain laughed a little.

"And she is going to search for a bit to go up there!" continued the girl more vehemently; and he laughed again.

"Yes," said Mary, "if you only saw something of her, you would be convinced that her whole character is very different from that of the rest of the family."

"Don't you be taken in by plausibility," said the captain. "I know that fellow Dan is a thief. I meant to tell his relation, George, that I won't allow him to be employed on the new schoolroom. I shall do so now."

"Would it not be better to forget what happened so long ago?" Mary ventured to say.

"And suppose Judith restores it," added Sophia.

"Pshaw!" said the captain; but Mary followed him to the study, and what she did with him there her sisters did not know, but it resulted in his allowing that Dan might have another trial, with a sharp eye over him.

So unused was Uphill to the visits of ladies, that when the piece of French paper was sold to Judith, no one had thought of her being sought out in her bedroom. Molly came home with the children in the evening, tired out but excited — for all had had rather more beer than was good for them, and the children a great many more sweets. Jem and Judy were quarrelling over a wooden horse covered with white spots, but whose mane had already disappeared, Lizzie was sick, cross, and stupid, Polly had broken the string of her new yellow necklace, and was crying about it, and nobody had recollected the aunt except Johnnie, who presented her with a piece of thin gingerbread representing King George the Fourth, in white, pink, and gilt! Molly herself was very tired, though she said it was all very fine, and she had seen a lot of people, and the big sleeves they wore were quite a wonder. Then she scolded Polly with all her might for crying and never setting the tea, nor boiling the kettle; and, after all, it was Johnnie who made up the fire, fetched water, and set the kettle boiling. They all wrangled together over their purchases, and the sights they had seen, or not seen, while Judith was glad to be out of the way of seeing, though not of hearing. Then the girls trailed themselves upstairs. Judy slept with her aunt, Polly and Lizzie had a kind of shake-down on a mattress of chaff or hulls, as she called it, by her side. Judith always insisted on their prayers, but they said they were much too tired tonight, and could not say anything but "Matthew, Mark, Luke, and John," which was all they knew except the Lord's Prayer. Judith had taught them this, but they thought the repeating it a very difficult ceremony, far too hard when they were tired.

Their mother went to bed soon afterwards, taking Jem with her, and so did Johnnie, all being anxious to get what sleep they could before the dreaded moment of father's return. Public-houses were not obliged to close at any special time in those days, and the homecoming, especially on a fair day, was apt to be a terrible affair. It was not till past one o'clock that shouts, broken bursts of singing, and howls of quarrelling announced the breakup of the riotous party, and presently the door bounced open, and with oaths at the darkness, though there was bright moonlight, Dan stumbled in and staggered upstairs, overturning the unlucky screen upon Polly as he did so, cursing and swearing at them all, and ordering his wife to get up and open the door, which he was past finding. He did not attack Judith, though he almost fell over her bed, and the two girls lay trembling, not daring to lift off the screen till the door of the bedroom was shut on them; and then came the only too well-known sound of their mother scolding and crying, and his swearing and beating her.

They were only too much used to such disturbance, and were asleep again before it was over; but Judith could only lie on, shaking with terror — not personal — but at the awful words she heard, and praying that they might not be visited on that unhappy household, but that God would forgive.

It was not till the next day when the house was tolerably quiet, and Molly, rather fretful and grumbling, had helped Judith down to her place by the fire, that she ventured the question, "Molly, you have not a bit more of that pretty wall-paper you gave me for my screen?"

"Did it get broke last night in Dan's drunken tantrums?"

"Not more than I can mend, but little Miss Sophia, she says that the paper in the Greenhow drawing-room is quite spoilt for want of a piece to cover up a bit that was put on wrong."

"My patience! And how did Miss Sophia come to know any-thing about it?"

"She came up to see me, and bring those cutlets that you are warming up now."

"Bless me! Well, Dan will be vexed," said Molly. "Such mean folk as they are, a-peeping and a-prying after every-thing! They knows how to look after whatever they chooses to say is their own; and the captain, he made a row before about that there trumpery yard or two of paper that was the parkisit of them that hung it."

"Miss Sophy says it spoilt the room."

"Sp'ilt it! They've little to vex 'em that is terrified about that!"

"But have you got the bit, Molly?"

"I never had it! Dan kept it in the outhouse. He may have a scrap left, that he used to make caps for the Christmas boys when he used the rest to paper Mrs. Hunter's closet with down at Downhill. Your piece was left over of that, and may be there was half-a-yard more; but he locks that there workshop of his, so as one can't get in to get a bit of shavings to light the fire. So you must ask him. I am sure I dare not do it. He's that angry if one does but look into his shop."

"I must try and get it!" said Judith.

"Not now, I wouldn't," entreated Molly. "What is it to the ladies? And father, he will be fit to tear the place down if he hears of it! Them Gobblealls is set again him already, and 'tis just taking away our bread to say a bit more about it to them folks. George Hewlett is particular enough already, without having a work about this."

Poor Judith, she felt as if she could never be at peace with her conscience, while she had those yellow laburnums in sight in her room, and she did not see how restitution and confession could injure her brother-in-law; but her code of right and wrong was very different from that of either husband or wife.

Molly went on maundering about the hardship of having taken in a poor helpless thing, and having stood between her and the workhouse, only that she should turn a viper and a spy, and take her poor children's bread out of their mouths, forgetting that Jem was at the very moment eating up the piece of apple pie that had come with the cutlets.

Judith tried to get her thoughts together, and decided that, however much she might dread Dan's anger, and care for his interest and family peace, it was her duty to do her best to recover whatever remnant was possible of his booty. So when he came home to dinner she ventured to ask him if he had a piece left of that paper of her screen.

"Why?" he asked, turning on her as if he hoped to make more of whatever he had.

She told him timidly, and it was as she had feared. He began abusing her violently for letting spies up into her room, and turning against him, that let her have her house-room, and "worriting" them all with her hypocritical ways. He could tell her there was nothing between her and the workhouse, and all was interspersed with oaths, terrible to hear.

Molly began taking her part, and declaring that Judith could not help it if little miss would come into her room; but Dan, who had qualified last night's revel with another mug of ale, was quite past all reason, and declared that Judith called the girl up on purpose to bring him into trouble, and that nothing but harm had ever come of her canting, Methody ways, and he had a good mind to kick her out at once to the workhouse, and would do so, if she brought them Gobblealls down on him again. There had been nothing but plague ever since they came into the parish, and he wouldn't have them come poll-prying about his house. No, he wouldn't.

Judith knew this was a vain threat, for he was always out of the house when they came, and she also knew that he was the last man to give up the small payment that she was in the habit of making quarterly, or what was begged from her besides, so she was not afraid of any such measure; but she was much shaken, and felt quite ill afterwards, and Molly did not stint her blame and lamentations. Nothing happened in consequence, except that, from that time forward, Dan's incipient dislike to "they Gobblealls" was increased, and they could do nothing which he did not find fault with; though his wife, grumbling at them all the time, was quite willing to get everything possible out of them.

CHAPTER X.

Innovations.

"Timotheus placed on high
Among the tuneful choir,
With flying fingers touched the lyre."
Dryden.

On the first of October the new beginning was to be made. The new curate, Mr. Harford, arrived, and spent his first few days at Greenhow, while looking out for a lodging at Downhill, for he was to be shared between the two parishes as before, and Mr. Atkins still undertook to assist on Sundays. Mr. Harford looked very young, almost a boy, and was small and thin, but not in the least delicate. He had only worked off his superfluous flesh in study and parish cares at Oxford, and he was likely to do the same in his new home. He looked on it as likely to be his residence for a long time, for, as the President had already told Mrs. Carbonel, he was engaged to a young lady, whose father would not consent to her marriage till he had a living worth 500 pounds a year, and there were a good many fellows senior to him.

He seemed to have no fears of any amount of work, and the first thing he thought of was how to arrange for Uphill to have two services on Sunday, as he thought could be contrived by giving the Downhill people, who mostly lived near the church, their second service in the evening instead of the morning; and, as Mr. Atkins would thus have more to do, he gave up to that gentleman the addition to his stipend, which the President had offered to himself. The boon was great to the Greenhow family, who had often been hindered by weather from getting to Downhill. Moreover, he had plans for one service and sermon in the week, and for a cottage lecture at a distant hamlet.

Also, in the first fortnight of his stay, he had called at every house, alike in Downhill and Uphill, to the great surprise of some of the families, who had not in the memory of man seen a parson cross their threshold. Some did not like it, such as old Dame Verdon, who, though she could hardly get out of bed, was very sore about the new school; and when her friends came to see her, told them wonderful stories which she had picked up — or Lizzie had from some hawker — that the gentlefolks thought there were too many children for the rates and taxes, and they were going to get them all into the school, and make an end of them. Sometimes she said it was by "giving of them all the cowpox," as Dame Spurrell called vaccination as the fashion was in those parts, sometimes it was by sending them all out to Botany Bay.

And as Mrs. Carbonel had prevailed on the new gardener's wife to have her baby vaccinated, and George Hewlett's and Mrs. Mole's children had been thence treated by her own hands, this was believed the more, although none of the children were visibly the worse for it after the first few days; but some of the women, and almost all the children believed the story, and many of the little ones were in fits of terror about the school, so that there was a falling off even with the Sunday School. The new school was only an additional room to a good-sized cottage, with a couple of windows and a brick floor, fitted with forms without backs, but which had at least good firm legs to stand upon, pegs for the cloaks and headgear round the walls, and a single desk, likely to be quite sufficient for the superior few who were to learn writing and summing. The stock, obtained from the Society for Promoting Christian Knowledge, consisted of a dozen copies of Mrs. Trimmer's Abridgment of the Old Testament, the same number of the lady's work on the New Testament, a packet of little paper books of the Sermon on the Mount, the Parables and the Miracles, and another packet of little books, where the alphabet led the way upwards from ba, bo, etc., to "Our cat can kill a rat; can she not?" Also the broken Catechism, and Sellon's Abridgment of instruction on the Catechism. There were a housewife full of needles, some brass thimbles, and a roll of calico provided, and this was the apparatus with which most village schools would commence.

Mrs. Thorpe arrived with her two little girls, the neatest of creatures, still wearing her weeds, as indeed widows engaged in any business used to do for life as a sort of protection. Under her crape borders showed the smoothest of hair, and her apron was spotlessly white. The two little girls were patterns, with short cut hair, spotted blue frocks and checkered pinafores in the week, lilac frocks on Sundays; white capes on that same day, and bonnets of coarse straw, tied down with green ribbon, over little bonnet caps with plain net frilling, the only attempt at luxury apparent in their dress. Their names were Jane and Mary, and they looked very pretty and demure, though there was a little mischief in Mary's eyes. Nothing could look nicer or more promising in the eyes of the sisters when they took her to her cottage, nor could any one be better pleased than she to work under her own young ladies, and to have so peaceful a home for her little daughters. She was introduced to her future scholars on Sunday in the wash-house, and very shy and awkward did they look, nor were the numbers as large as usual.

Mr. Harford came to open the school on Monday morning, and the ladies met him there. The room was in beautiful order, and presently the younger Moles, the George Hewletts, the Seddons, the Pucklechurch grandchildren, and about half-a-dozen more dropped in; but no one else appeared, and these stood handling their pennies and looking sheepish.

Mr. Harford, after looking out to see whether any one else was coming, addressed them in words a little too fine for their comprehension, and then read a few prayers, after which he and Mrs. Carbonel went away, taking the unwilling Sophy to her lessons, but leaving Dora to follow when she had heard the names called over, and inaugurated the work; and their journey was enlivened by meeting a child with flying hair and ragged garments rushing headlong, so as to have only just time to turn off short over a gap in a field where some men who were ploughing called out, "Run, little one, run; she'll catch thee!" with a great shouting laugh, and at the same moment appeared, with a big stick in her hand, Nancy Morris in full chase, her cap on the back of her head, and looking not much less wild than her offspring.

However, she drew up at the sight of the clergyman and

the lady, pulled her cap forward and her apron to the middle, curtsied low, and in a voice of conscious merit, though out of breath, explained that she was "arter Elizabeth," who was that terrifying and contrary that she would not go to school.

Mr. Harford, not quite accustomed to the popular use of the verb to terrify, began to ask what the child had done to alarm her mother so much and Nancy, understanding him as little, said, "'Tis all along of Dame Verdon, ma'am. She be for to say that the new governess will beat them and send them off to Minsterham, as sure as they're alive; and I told Bet not to believe no such stuff, but her won't listen to I — "

Mr. Harford was the more mystified. Why should she send them to Minsterham? And what was the child afraid of? Mrs. Carbonel had more notion. Minsterham was the assize town, and going thither was a polite form of mentioning the being before a court of justice.

"Elizabeth need have no fears of a prison," she said. "She is a silly child to be frightened; but when she sees that the other children like school, and that nothing happens to them, she will know better. Don't beat her, it will only frighten her more."

"If it is your will, ma'am, I'll let her off; but I'll give her the stick another time, as sure as she is alive, the little toad."

"Hopeful," said the lady and gentleman to each other, as soon as she was out of sight, and they could laugh.

It was indeed uphill work in every sense that was before Mrs. Thorpe, but the effect was visible in much improvement in the general demeanour of the children. A chair was found for her where she sat among them at church, and prevented the outrageous misconduct that the ladies had been unable effectively to check; and the superior readers were gradually acquiring a very cheap form of Prayer-book, with only Matins and Evensong and the Collects, besides the Psalms.

But that the children sat on the chancel steps, and that kneeling in church was unknown to them, never occurred as an irreverence to any of the party, though as Mr. Harford read the ante-Communion service from the altar instead of disrobing himself of his surplice in the pulpit just before the sermon, he had to walk through the whole school, making those in his way stand up to let him pass.

The singers, on the establishment of a double service, began to absent themselves at least once on a Sunday, so Mr. Harford and the ladies tried to arrange for the singing of the children instead. He had no knowledge of music, which was then thought a rather doubtful accomplishment for a young man, and Mrs. Thorpe had, if possible, less, so all that could be done was for Dora to train the children by ear; and she found that their thin, shrill notes were held as painful by all save a few doting mothers, her sisters, and herself. The captain laughed at her, and finally promised her a grinding organ. It came; it could play four tunes, and all the singers were naturally offended. But on the first Sunday there was a great catastrophe, for when once set on it would not stop, but went on playing its four tunes long after the Old Hundredth was finished. Mr. Harford waited to begin the Prayer for King George till it had finished, hoping that it would stop, if not at the end of the second tune at least at the fourth; but, behold, it started off with the Old Hundredth again, upon which Captain Carbonel emerged from his pew, and, with the help of Master Pucklechurch, bore it out into the churchyard, where it continued to play till after the service, when there was time to check its pertinacity by adjustment of the machinery. At its best, the singers — even George Hewlett — were much hurt, and the compromise was made that it never should uplift its voice when they were present in full force with bass, flute, and viol, but should only draw forth its four tunes when there were only the children to need the accompaniment.

Even then, Dan Hewlett, who unluckily had the best voice of all, swore that he would never come to church again while "they had that there horgin to buzz away like a big bumbledore;" and he kept his word.

"You see, ma'am, he has his feelings," said Molly.

He would fain have made all his family join in the secession; but Johnnie would not be kept away from Sunday School; and Molly had heard rumours of penny clubs and of prizes at Christmas so, though the other children were very irregular, she kept them on after a fashion.

CHAPTER XI.

An Unprofitable Crop.

"My mother bids me bind my hair."
— *Old Ballad.*

"Oh Mary, Mary, what is to be done about the hair?" cried Sophy, one Sunday after church.

"Isn't it dreadful?" said Dora. "Those fearful curl-papers sticking out with rolls of old newspapers! I told them it was not fit to be seen last Sunday, but there were even Elizabeth and Jane Hewlett in them today."

"Yes," said Mary, "they said that mother's aunt was coming to tea, so she had curled them before they came out. I told them I would excuse it for this once, but that I should send any one home who came such a figure on Sunday."

Elizabeth and Jane, be it observed, were George Hewlett's daughters, the most civilised, if the dullest-witted, of the flock. Polly, Betsy, and Judy were the children of Dan Hewlett. As a rule, all the old women of the parish were called Betty, all the middle-aged Lizzie, and the girls Elizabeth.

"It is worse on weekdays," said Dora. "One would think it was a collection of little porcupines!"

"And so dirty," began Sophy, but she was hushed up, for Edmund was seen approaching, and Mary never allowed him to be worried with the small, fretting details of school life.

It was a time when it was the fashion for young ladies up to their teens to have their hair curled in ringlets round their heads or on their shoulders. Sophy's hair curled naturally, and had been "turned up" ever since she had come to live at home in the dignity of fourteen, but she and both her sisters wore falls of drooping ringlets in front, and in Mary's case these had been used to be curled in paper at night, though she would as soon have been seen thus decorated by day as in her nightcap. But there was scarcely another matron in the parish who did not think a fringe of curl-paper the proper mode of disposing of her locks when in morning désabillé, unless she were elderly and wore a front, which could be taken off and put on with the best cap.

Maid-servants wore short curls or smooth folds round side-combs under net caps, and this was the usual trim of the superior kind of women. The working women wore thick muslin white caps, under which, it was to be hoped, their hair was cut short, though often it straggled out in unseemly elf-locks. Married women did not go bareheaded, not even the younger ladies, except in the evening, when, like their maiden sisters, they wore coils of their back hair round huge upright ornamental combs on the summit of their heads.

But the children's heads were deservedly pain and grief to the Carbonel senses, and Mary was impelled to go and make a speech in school, desiring that no more curl-papers should appear there on Sundays, and recommending that all hair should be kept short, as her own and her sister's had been, till the fit age for the "turning up" was attained. She called up Susan Pucklechurch and Rachel Mole, who had nice smooth hair neatly parted in the middle, and declared them to be examples of the way that heads ought to appear.

That afternoon the women stood out at their gates. "So the lady told you to take pattern by Widdy Mole's child, did her?" said Nanny Barton, loud enough for all her neighbours to hear.

"Ay, mother, by Rachel Mole and Susie Pucklechurch."

"As if I'd go out of my way to follow after a mean creeper and low thing like Widow Mole," exclaimed Mrs. Barton.

"She knows which way her bread is buttered. A-making favourites!" exclaimed Nancy Morris.

"Getting in to work in the garding away from Farmer Goodenough, as her man had worked for for years, ay, and his before un," chimed in Nanny Barton.

"And if you could see the platefuls and cupfuls as the ladies carries out to her," added Betsy Seddon. "My word and honour! No wonder she is getting lively enough just to bust some day."

"That's the way she comes over them," said Nanny Barton.

"That's what them gentlefolks likes, and Bessy Mole she

knows it," observed Nancy Morris; at which they all laughed shrilly.

"As though I'd take pattern by her," exclaimed Nanny Barton. "I'd liefer take pattern by Softy Sam, or Goodenough's old scarecrow."

"Whatever's that?" demanded Tirzah, coming out of the "Fox and Hounds." "What have they been after now?"

"Just the lady's been a preachin' down at that there school, how that she don't want no curl-papers there, and that all the poor children's heads is to be clipped like boys, and setting up that there Rachel Mole's bowl-dish of a poll to set the fashion."

"There! As I told you," said Tirzah. "That's the way gentry always goes on if they gets their way."

"They just hates to see a curl or a bit of ribbon," added Betsy Seddon.

"Or to see one have a bit of pleasure," added Nancy Morris. "Pucklechurches and Mole, they never durst send their poor children to the fair —"

"And to hear the lady run out agin' me for just having a drop of beer," exclaimed Nanny Barton. "Nothing warn't bad enough for me! As if she hadn't her wine and all the rest of it, and a poor woman mayn't touch one draught, if it is ever so —"

"Well, you know, Nan, you'd had a bit more than enough," said Tirzah.

"Well, and what call to that was hern or yourn?" cried Nancy, facing upon her.

"A pretty job I had to get you home that night," said Tirzah; and they all laughed. "And you wouldn't be here now if Tom Postboy hadn't pulled up his horses in time."

"And was it for her to cast up to me if I was a bit over-taken?" demanded Nanny.

It may be supposed that after such a conversation as this there was not much chance of the bowl-dish setting the fashion. There was not the same ill-temper and jealousy of Susan Pucklechurch being held up as an example, for her family were the natural hangers-on of Greenhow, and were, besides, always neater and better dressed than the others; but Mrs. Mole was even poorer than themselves, and had worked with them, even while "keeping herself to herself," a great offence in their eyes. Thus nobody was inclined to follow the clipped fashion, except one or two meeker women, who had scarcely seen that their girls' hair was getting beyond bounds. It is to be remembered that seventy years ago, long hair could hardly be kept in respectable trim by busy mothers working in the fields, and with much less power of getting brushes and combs than at present; so that the crops were almost the only means of securing cleanliness and tidiness, and were worn also by all the little daughters of such gentry as did not care for fashion, nor for making them sleep on a ring of lumps as big as walnuts. So that Mrs. Carbonel and her sisters really wished for what was wholesome and proper when they tried to make the children conform to their rules, if the women could only have seen it so, instead of resenting the interference.

Sunday brought George Hewlett's two girls with their hair fastened up in womanly guise, and their cousins becurled as before; but there was nothing particularly untidy, and Mary held her peace.

However, the war was not over, and one day, when, after a short absence, Dora and Sophy went into the school, they found five or six girls bristling with twists of old newspapers, and others in a still more objectionable condition, with wild unkempt hair about their necks, and the half-dozen really neat ones were on the form around Mrs. Thorpe, who proceeded to tell Dora that she was quite in despair, the more she spoke to the girls about tidy heads, the worse they were, and she was really afraid to let her own children or the clean ones sit near the dirty ones.

Dora's spirit was roused. "Very well," she said, "Mrs. Carbonel and I will not be disobeyed. Come here, Lizzie Barton. Your head is disgraceful. Lend me your scissors, Mrs. Thorpe."

Lizzie Barton began to cry, with her knuckles in her eyes, and would not stir; but Dora was resolute. One child made a rush for the door; but Dora desired Sophy to stand by the door and bar the passage, and called Mrs. Thorpe to hold Lizzie Barton, who certainly was a spectacle, with half-a-dozen horns twisted out of old advertisement papers, but the rest of her hair flying in disgusting elf-locks. She was cowed, however, into standing quiet, till her appendages had been sheared off by the determined scissors. "There, I am sure you must be much more comfortable," Dora assured her. "Get your mother to wash your head, and you will look so nice tomorrow. Now then, Betsy Hewlett."

Betsy cried, but submitted; but the next victim, Sally French, howled and fought, and said, "Mammy would not have it done." But Dora sternly answered, "Then she should keep your head fit to be seen." And Mrs. Thorpe held down her hands, with whispers of "Now, my dear, don't."

And so it went on through nineteen girls, the boys sniggering all the time. Some cried and struggled, but latterly they felt it was their fate, and resisted no longer. Even Mary Cox, who had a curly head by nature, stood still to be clipped. Dora's hands were in a dreadful state, and her mind began to quail a little; but, having once started, she felt bound to go on and complete her work, and when she finally dismissed the school, there was a very undesirable heap of locks, brown, black, and carroty, interspersed with curl-papers, on the floor. The girls looked, to her mind, far better, and Mrs. Thorpe, a little doubtful, gave her a basin of water to wash her hands.

Home the two sisters went, their spirits rising as they laughed over their great achievement, and looked forward to amusing Mary with the account of the various behaviour of the victims.

So they burst upon her, as she was planting bulbs in the garden, and Edmund helping her by measuring distances.

"Oh, Mary, such fun!" cried Sophy. "We have been cutting all the children's hair."

"What do you mean, Sophy?"

"They had their heads worse than ever," said Dora, "so I took Mrs. Thorpe's scissors and clipped them all round."

"My dear Dora, I wish you had not been so hasty," Mary was gently saying; but Edmund was standing up, looking quite judicial.

"Did you get their parents' permission?" he demanded.

"No, of course I never should."

"Then what right had you to meddle with the children?"

"They were quite horrid. My hands! They'll never recover," said Dora, spreading out her fingers.

"Very likely; but the children were not your slaves. You have a perfect right to forbid them to enter your school except on certain conditions, but not to tyrannise over them when there. You have done more harm than you will undo in a hurry."

"I am afraid so," murmured Mary.

Dora had a temper, and answered angrily, "Well, I'm sure I did it for the best."

"I don't approve of opinionative young ladies," said Edmund, who was really from old habit quite like an elder brother.

"Oh, Dora," sighed Mary, "don't!"

Dora felt impelled to argue the matter out on the spot, but something in Mary's look withheld her. She went away, stepping high and feeling stately and proud; but when she had walked up and down her own room a few times, her better sense began to revive, and she saw that she had acted in anger and self-will quite as much as from a sense of propriety, and she threw herself on her bed and shed some bitter tears.

They would have been still more bitter if she could have heard the exclamations of the mothers over their gates that evening.

"Well, to be sure, that a young lady should have treated my poor like that!"

"Her father says, says he, 'I'll have the law of she.'"

"My Jenny, she come home looking like a poor mad woman. 'Whatever has thee been arter?' says I. ''Tis the lady,' says she."

"Lady! She ought to be ashamed on herself, a-making such Betties of the poor children."

"Ah! didn't I tell you," gibed Tirzah, "what would come of making up to the gentlefolk, with their soft words and such. They only want to have their will of you, just like the blackamoors."

"You'll not find me a sending my Liz and Nan," cried Mrs. Morris, "no, not if her was to offer me a hundred goulden guineas."

"I don't let my gal go to be made into a guy!" was the general sentiment; and Mrs. Verdon, in her bed, intensified it by warning her neighbours that the cropping their heads was "a preparation for sending them out to them foreign parts where they has slaves."

And on Sunday, there were only ten of the female pupils at school, and poor Dora and Sophia both cried all church time. They thought their hasty measures had condemned their poor girls to be heathens and good-for-nothings for ever and ever.

Tirzah Todd laughed at them all. The Todds had gipsy connections; Todd himself was hardly ever visible. He was never chargeable to the parish, but he never did regular work except at hay and harvest times, or when he was cutting copsewood. Then old Pucklechurch's brother, Master Pucklechurch of Downhill, who always managed the copse cutting, used to hire him, and they and another man lived in a kind of wigwam made of chips, and cut down the seven years' growth of underwood, dividing it into pea-sticks from the tops, and splitting the thicker parts to be woven into hurdles, or made into hoops for barrels. They had a little fire, but their wives brought them their food, and little Hoglah, now quite well only with a scarred neck, delighted to toddle about among the chips, and cry out, "Pitty! pitty!" at the primroses.

Copse cutting over, Joe Todd haunted fairs and drove cattle home, or did anything he could pick up. He lived in a mud hovel which he and Tirzah had built for themselves on the border land, and where they kept a tall, thin, smooth-haired dog, with a grey coat, a white waistcoat, a long nose and tail, and blue eyes, which gave him a peculiarly sinister expression of countenance, and he had a habit of leaping up and planting his fore feet on the gate, growling, so that Dora and Sophy were very much afraid of him, and no one except Mr. Harford had ever attempted to effect an entrance into the cottage. It was pretty well understood that Joe Todd and his lurcher carried on a business as poachers, and Tirzah going about with clothes'-pegs, rush baskets, birch brooms, and in their season with blackberries, whortleberries, or plovers' eggs, was able to dispose of their game to the poulterers at Minsterham, with whom she had an understanding. Her smiling black eyes, white teeth, and merry looks, caused a great deal of business to be done through her, and servants were not unwilling to carry in her stories about rabbits knocked down unawares by a stick, and pheasants or partridges killed by chance in reaping. Indeed, she had a little trade in dripping and other scraps with sundry of these servants, which rendered them the more disposed to receive her.

CHAPTER XII.

Prizes.

"Miss Jenny and Polly
Had each a new dolly,
   With rosy red cheeks and blue eyes,
Dressed in ribbons and gauze;
And they quarrelled because
   The dolls were not both of a size."

The Daisy.

Nobody offered a hundred golden guineas to bring Elizabeth and Anne Morris to school, nevertheless they appeared there at the end of the second week. They were heartily tired of home, where there was washing to be done, and their eldest sister Patty banged them about, and they had no peace from the great heavy baby. Besides, there had been a talk of prizes at Christmas, and they weren't going to let them Moles and Pucklechurches get the whole of them. Moreover, others were going back, so why should not they?

Yes, Nanny Barton's children "did terrify her so, she had no peace." And Betsy Seddon's Janie had torn her frock as there was no bearing, and even the Dan Hewletts were going back. Little Judy had cried to go, and her Aunt Judith had trimmed up the heads of her sisters, for Dora Carbonel had not been a first-rate hair-cutter, and it was nearly the same with every one, except the desperate truant, Ben Shales, and the cobbler's little curly girl, who was sent all the way to Downhill to Miss Minifer's genteel academy, where she learnt beadwork and very little besides.

The affair seemed to have done less harm than Captain Carbonel had expected, yet, on the other hand, the motives that brought most of the scholars back were not any real desire for improvement, but rather the desire of being interested, and the hope of rewards. It would take a long time to make the generality of the people regard "they Gobblealls" as anything but curious kind of creatures to be humoured for the sake of what could be got out of them.

Of the positive love of God and their neighbour, and the strong sense of duty that actuated them, few of the Uphill inhabitants had the least notion. It would be much to say that if these motives were always present with Edmund and Mary, it was so in the same degree with Dora and Sophy; but to them the school children were the great interest, occupation, and delight, and their real affection and sympathy, so far as they understood, were having their effect.

They were hard at work at those same prizes, which filled almost as much of their minds as they could those of the expectant recipients, and occupied their fingers a good deal. And, after all, what would the modern scholar think of those same prizes? The prime ones of all, the Bible and Prayer-book, were of course, in themselves as precious then as now, but each was bound in the very plainest of dark-brown calf, though, to tell the truth, far stronger than their successors, and with the leaves much better sewn in. There was only one of each of these, for Susan Pucklechurch and Johnnie Hewlett, who were by far the foremost scholars in the Sunday School.

Then followed two New Testaments and two Psalters, equally brown, for the next degree. Sophy had begged for stories, but none were to be had within the appointed sum, except Hannah More's Cheap Repository Tracts, really interesting, but sent forth without wrappers in their native black and white. Then there was a manufacture by the busy fingers, frocks made of remnants of linsey and print, of sun-bonnets of pink or blue spotted calico, of pinafores, and round capes, the least of all these being the list tippet, made of the listing of flannel, sewn on either in rays upon a lining, or in continued rows from the neck, leaving rather the effect of a shell. There were pin-cushions, housewives, and work-bags too, and pictured pocket-handkerchiefs, and Sophy would not be denied a few worsted balls for the very small boys, and sixpennyworth of wooden dolls for the lesser girls, creatures with painted faces, and rolls of linen for arms, nailed on to bodies that ended in a point, but all deficiencies were concealed by the gay print petticoats which she constructed, and as neither toys, nor the means of buying them were plentiful, these would be grand rewards.

The Christmas-tree had not yet begun to spring in England, magic lanterns were tiny things only seen in private, and even such festivities as the tea had not dawned on the scholastic mind. So, on the afternoon of Christmas Day, all the children were assembled in school before Mr. Harford, the ladies, and the schoolmistress, while the table was loaded with books and garments, and beside it stood a great flasket brimming over with substantial currant buns, gazed on eagerly by the little things, some of whom had even had a scanty Christmas dinner. Such a spectacle had never been seen before in Uphill, and their hungry eyes devoured it beforehand.

Mr. Harford made them a short speech about goodness, steadiness, and diligence, and then the distribution began with the two prime Sunday scholars, and went on in due order of merit, through all degrees, down to the mites who had the painted dolls, and figured handkerchiefs with Aesop's fables in pink or in purple, and then followed the distribution of buns, stout plum buns, no small treat to these ever hungry children, some of whom were nibbling them before they were out of school, while others, more praiseworthy, kept them to share with "our baby" at home.

Johnnie Hewlett received a Bible, his sister Polly a warm cape, Lizzie a petticoat, little Judy a doll, but on the very last Sunday, Jem, always a black sheep, had been detected in kicking Jenny Morris at church over a screw of peppermint drops which they had clubbed together to purchase from Goody Spurrell. The scent and Jenny's sobs had betrayed them in the thick of the combat, and in the face of so recent and so flagrant a misdemeanour, neither combatant could be allowed a prize, though the buns were presented to them through Mary's softness of heart.

These stayed the tears for the moment, but a fresh shower was pumped up by Jem for the sympathetic reception of his mother. "It was a shame! it was; but they ladies always had a spite at the poor little lad. He should have some nice bull's-eyes to make up to him, that he should! What call had they to be at him when it was all along of that there nasty little Jenny."

Nevertheless, at the gate she shared her wrath with Jenny's mother. What call had they to want to make the poor children to be like parsons at church? Jem shouldn't be there no more, she could tell them.

Then Nanny Barton chimed in. "And look what they did give! Just a twopenny-halfpenny handkercher that her Tom would be ashamed to wear!"

He wasn't, for it was thick and warm, and had been chosen because his poor little neck looked so blue. But Molly went on. "Ladies did ought to know what became 'em to give. There was my Lady Duchess, she gave 'em all scarlet cloaks, and stuff frocks, as there was some warmth in. That was worth having — given to all alike! No talk of prizes, for what I'd not demean myself to pick up out of the gutter."

"And look at mine," proceeded Molly. "My Johnnie's got a Bible, as if there wasn't another in the house, let alone Judith's. His father, he did say he'd pawn it; but Johnnie he cried, and Judith made a work, and hid it for him. But his father, he says he wouldn't have Johnnie made religious, not for nothing — Judith she's quite bad enough."

"Oh! our Polly — she got a little skimping cape, what don't come down to her poor little elbows. If I went for to be a lady, I'd be ashamed to give the like of that."

Happily every one did not receive the gifts in this spirit. There was much rejoicing over the Testament, frock, and Psalter of the little Moles, and their grandfather observed, "Well, you did ought to be good children, there were no such encouragements when I was young."

"Except your big old Bible, granfer," put in Bessy.

"That was give me by our old parson when me and your granny was married. Ay, he did catechise we in church when we was children, but we never got nothing for it."

"Only the knowing it, father, and that you have sent on to us," put in the widow.

"Ay, and that's the thing!" said the old man, very gravely.

CHAPTER XIII.

Against the Grain.

"And shall the heirs of sinful blood
Find joy unmixed in charity?"
Keble.

These first beginnings were really hard work, and there was a great amount of unpopularity to be encountered, for the people of Uphill were so utterly unused to kindness that they could not believe that anything was done for them from disinterested motives. Captain Carbonel took great trouble to set up a coal club, persuading the President of Saint Cyril's and the neighbouring landowners to subscribe, and the farmers to fetch the coal on the plea that to have fuel on low terms would save the woods and hedges from destruction. Tirzah especially, and half-a-dozen women besides were to be met with great faggots of limbs of trees on their backs from Mr. Selby's woods, and the keepers were held to wink at it, for, in truth, the want of fuel was terrible. Mr. Selby talked of withholding his yearly contribution of blankets, because the people were so ungrateful. "As if it would do them any good to make them colder," cried Dora.

So at last it was arranged that one of the barns should be filled with coal, and Captain Carbonel and Mr. Harford, with old Pucklechurch, were to see it served out at sixpence a bushel every Monday morning. And then, Pucklechurch reported that the people said, "Depend on it, the captain made a good thing of it." So, when he divided one of his fields into allotment gardens, for those who had portions too scanty for the growth of their potatoes, though he let them off at a rate which brought in rent below the price of land in the parish, the men were ready enough to hire them, but they followed Dan Hewlett's lead in believing that "that Gobbleall knew what he was about, and made a good thing of it"; while the farmers, like Mr. Goodenough, were much displeased, declaring that the allotments would only serve as an excuse for pilfering. Truly, whatever good was attempted in Uphill, had to be done against the stream, for nobody seemed to be on the side of the Carbonels except Mr. Harford, and a few of the poor, such as the old Pucklechurches, Widow Mole and her father, the George Hewletts, and poor Judith Grey, besides all the better children, who were easily won.

It made the more difficulty that though Captain Carbonel was a patient man in deed, did not set his expectations too high, and bore, in fact, with an amazing amount of disappointment and misunderstanding; yet he was not patient in word, and was apt to speak very sharply when indignant with cruelty, shuffling, or what was more unlucky, with stupidity. The men used to declare that he swore at them, which was perfectly untrue, for a profane word never crossed his lips, but when he was very angry, he spoke in a tone that perhaps might excuse them for thinking that his reproofs were flavoured as had been the abuse to which they were only too well accustomed.

The tormentors of poor Softy Sam always slunk out of reach at the most distant report of the approach of the captain, the curate, or the ladies, but the men never understood their objections to the sport that had hitherto been freely afforded by the idiot, and had a general idea that the gentlefolk disliked whatever afforded them amusement.

George Hewlett, indeed, knew better; but then he had never joined in baiting Softy Sam, and, indeed, had more than once sheltered him from his enemies, and given him a bit of food. But George in his own line was dull and unapt to learn; or the whole adventure of the Greenhow drawing-room paper would never have happened. He might have had it put up wrongly, for that was wholly the defect of his perceptions, but Dan would not have been able to secure his unlawful gains. In fact, Dan had traded on his cousin's honest straightforward blindness and stupidity a good many times already.

Captain Carbonel stormed at George when he failed to understand directions, or cut a bit of wood to waste; but without loss of confidence, and before long, Master Hewlett came to accept it as the captain's way, and to trust him as a really kind and liberal employer. And, unluckily, he did not always heed the rating so loudly given, or rather he did not set his mind to comprehend what lay a little out of his usual beat, and thus gave additional provocation, though still Captain Carbonel bore with him, and would not have rejected him in favour of the far smarter carpenter at Downhill, on any of these provocations.

Dan, who was a much sharper fellow, could have helped a great deal, but his back was up at the first word, and he would do nothing but sulk. Moreover, George himself detected him doing away with some wood out of that which was to make Farmer Goodenough's farm gates, under colour that it was a remnant only fit for firewood. Having already announced that he would never again employ his cousin after another of these peculations, he kept to his word, and in spite of Molly's tears and abuse, and Dan's deeper objurgations, he persisted. Daniel tried to get work at Downhill, but all the time declared that them Gobblealls was at the bottom of it, having a spite at him.

Just at this time Captain Carbonel was driving the phaeton, with his wife in it, home from Elchester; when, just as they were passing Todd's house, a terrible scream was heard. Shrieks that did not mean naughtiness but agony; and a flame was visible within the door. In one moment the captain was over the wicket, past the lurcher, dragging with him his great old military cloak, which had been over Mary's knees. Another second, and he had wrapped little Hoglah in it from top to toe, stifling the flames by throwing her down and holding her tight, while her mother came flying in from the garden; and Mary, throwing the reins of the horse to the servant, hurried in.

Tirzah was screaming and sobbing. "My child! My dear! Oh, Hoggie! Hoggie! Is she dead! Oh!"

"No, no; I think not," said the captain. And, indeed, no sooner did he begin to unroll her than cries broke out, very sufficient answer as to the child's being alive, and as her mother vehemently clasped her they grew more agonising.

"Let me see how much she is burnt," said Mrs. Carbonel.

"You had better not squeeze her. It makes it worse."

The child's poor little neck and bosom proved to have been sadly burnt. Her mother had been heating the oven, and had gone out to fetch fresh faggots, when the little one, trying in baby-fashion to imitate the proceedings, had set her pinafore on fire. Many more children were thus destroyed than now, when they do not wear so much cotton, nor such long frocks and pinafores.

Poor little Hoglah screamed and moaned terribly, and the thought of her being unbaptised came with a shock across Mrs. Carbonel. However, she did not think the injuries looked fatal, and speaking gently to soothe the mother, as she saw the preparations for baking, she said, "I think we can give her a little ease, my dear, my dear."

Tirzah was sobbing, screaming, and calling on her dear child, quite helpless at the moment, while Mary took the moaning child. Captain Carbonel, with his own knife (finding it more effective than the blunt old knife on the table), cut off the remains of the little garments which had become tinder, and then handed his wife the flour in a sort of scoop, and as she sprinkled it over the burnt surface, the shrieks and moans abated and gradually died away, the child muttered, "Nice, nice," and another word or two, which her mother understood as asking for something to drink. Beer, to Mary's dismay, was the only thing at hand, but after a sup of that, the little thing's black eyes closed, and she said something of "Mammy," and "Bye, bye." The great old cradle stood by, still used, though the child was three years old, and Mrs. Carbonel laid her carefully in it.

"I think she will get well," said she to the mother, "only you must not let the flour be disturbed on any account." She had arranged handkerchiefs, her own, and a red one of Tirzah's, to cover the dressing. "I will send you some milk, and don't let the coverings be disturbed. Let her lie; only give her milk when she wants it, and I will come to see her tomorrow."

Tirzah was sobbing quietly now, but she got out a choked question as to whether the child could get well.

"Oh yes; no fear of that, if you let the flour alone, as Mrs.

Carbonel tells you," said the captain.

"Oh, oh! if it wasn't for you — " the mother began.

But Edmund wanted to get his wife away before there was a scene, and cut it short with, "There, there! We'll come again. Only let her alone, and don't meddle with the flour."

Tirzah did what no native of Uphill would have thought of. She clasped Mrs. Carbonel's hand, threw herself on her knees, and kissed it.

"Thank God, not me," said Mary, much moved. "But you will give her to God now, and let her be baptized. I think she will live, but it ought to be as God's child."

When the curate came in a little later, to hear how the child was, Tirzah allowed him to baptize her privately. It might partly have been the dread of missing the Burial Service, but far more because in this present mood she was ready to do anything for madam.

Even when the neighbours thronged in, and Mrs. Spurrell wanted to take the child up, pull off the flour, and anoint her with oil and spirit, she would not hear of it.

"They as saved her shall have their will of her," said she.

"Saved her! She'll sleep herself off to death! What's the good of simple stuff like that, with no sting nor bite in it?" said Nanny Barton.

"Ay," said Mrs. Spurrell, "this ile as my great-aunt gave me, as they said was a white witch, with all her charrums, is right sovereign! Why, I did Jenny Truman's Sally with it when her arm was burnt."

"Ay, and you could hear her holler all over the place," said Tirzah; "and she've no use of her arm, poor maid! No, you shan't touch my child no how."

Tirzah kept her word, and Mrs. Carbonel came every day and doctored the child, and Sophy brought her a doll, which kept her peaceful for hours. The lurcher never barked at them, but seemed to understand their mission. And a wonderful old gipsy grandmother of Tirzah's, with eyes like needles and cheeks like brown leather, came and muttered charms over the child, and believed her cure was owing to them; but she left a most beautiful basket, white and purple, for a present to the lady.

CHAPTER XIV.

An Offer Rejected.

"Oft in Life's stillest shade reclining
In desolation unrepining,
Without a hope on earth to find
A mirror in an answering mind,
Meek souls there are who little deem
Their daily strife an angel's theme."

Keble.

In the spring Dora was invited to spend a few weeks with an old family friend in London, where there were daughters who had always been her holiday friends, and with whom she exchanged letters, on big square pages of paper, filled to the very utmost with small delicate handwriting, crossed over so that they looked like chequer-work, and going into all the flaps and round the seal. They did not come above once in a month or six weeks, and contained descriptions of what the damsels had seen, thought, heard, read, or felt; so that they were often really worth the eightpence that had to be paid on their reception.

Edmund, who had business in London, took his sister-in-law there, driving old Major to the crossroads, where they met the stagecoach. He went outside, on the box-seat, and she in the dull and close-packed interior, where four persons and one small child had to make the best of their quarters for the six hours that the journey lasted. Tired, headachy, and dusty with March dust, at last Dora emerged, and was very glad to rattle through the London streets in a hackney coach to Mr. Elwood's tall house, where there was a warm welcome ready for her.

But we need not hear of the pictures she saw, nor the music she heard, nor the plays she enjoyed, nor the parties she went to during that thorough holiday — though perhaps some would not call it a holiday, since the morning was spent in lessons in music, drawing, and Italian, in practising these same lessons, and in reading history aloud — the reading of some lighter book being an evening pleasure when the family were alone. Dora would not have enjoyed it half so much if it had not been for the times of real solid thought and interest. Her friends, too, had some poems still in manuscript lent to them, which made an immense impression on the young souls, and which they all learnt and discussed on Sundays, trying to enter into their meaning, and insensibly getting moulded by them. They were the poems that Dora knew a few years later as the "Christian Year." They made her home-work still dearer to her, and she had never let her interest fade among all her pleasures, but she was accumulating little gifts for the children, for Betty Pucklechurch, Widow Mole, Judith Grey, and the rest.

One day, when some intimate friends of the Elwoods were spending the day with them, something was said about Dora's home; and one of the visitors exclaimed, "Uphill — Uphill, near Poppleby, — is that the place?"

"Yes."

"Then I wonder whether you can tell me anything about our dear old nursery maid, Judith Grey."

"Judith Grey! Oh yes! She is the very nicest person in all Uphill," cried Dora. "Is it your father that gives her a pension?"

"Yes. You know it was while carrying little Selina downstairs, that she put her foot into the string of James's humming-top, and tumbled down all the stone stairs. She managed to save Selina — dear old Judy! — but she hurt her back most dreadfully, and she can't ever be well again, so papa gives her an allowance. She writes cheerfully, but we should like to hear more about her. We all were so fond of her."

"Indeed, I don't wonder. She is so good and patient. Such a dear thing! Mary and I call her the bright spot in our parish."

"She lives with a sister, I think. Is she nice?"

Dora had her opportunity, and she painted Dan Hewlett and his household in no flattering colours. Molly was a slattern, and Dan was a thief, and the children ate up Judith's dainties, and they all preyed upon her. It was a perfectly horrid life for a good, well-trained, high-principled person to lead. In fact, she poured out all the indignant accusations that she and Mary had been wont to make between themselves or to Edmund; and she sent Caroline and Anne Barnard home greatly shocked at what she had told them of their dear Judy's surroundings.

Mrs. Barnard came the next day, and begged to hear Miss Carbonel's account. Dora was a little more moderate than she had been to the young ladies; but, any way, it was sad enough, and Mrs. Barnard gave hopes that something should be done. All the family sent little presents of books or articles of dress, and Dora promised to write and let her know of their reception.

It was one of the great pleasures of the return to spread them out before Judith, and to tell of her sight of the dear young ladies and their mother, and how tall, and what a fine girl little Miss Selina had become. But she did not seem quite so happy when she perceived that Dora had disclosed a good deal of her circumstances; and observed that her sister was always a good sister to her. Which Dora took leave to doubt, especially when she recognised Miss Barnard's pretty gift of a blue turnover, all on one side, upon young Polly's dirty shoulders. Judith waited, and hoped, and gave up hope, and found fault with the Barnards before she heard anything; but at last she did. The Barnards' old housekeeper, with whom Judith had lived, had married their head gardener. He had died, and she was settled in a cottage in the park, where she would be very happy to receive Judith, and make her comfortable. The place was only thirty miles off, and if she consented, Mrs. Barnard would pay a visit she had been asked to make to the Duchess, and take Judith back in the easy carriage, so as to spare her all fatigue.

Dora and Sophy were in a state of transport, and wanted to rush off at once with the good news, but Mary withheld them. She thought it might be too much for so frail an invalid, and insisted on going with them and telling Judith herself. Nor would she go till after Sophy's morning studies were over, and they had had luncheons which, by-the-by, was not an early dinner, but a slender meal of cold meat, cake, or bread and cheese, of which Edmund never partook at all. She devised this delay on purpose to wear down the excitement, and Dora had begun to say how they should miss Judith, only it was all for her good.

Molly was out, as the sisters hoped, tossing the meadow hay, and Judith sat alone by the fire. Mary told her very gently of the scheme, and she kept on saying, "Thank you, ma'am," while the tears came into her eyes. Mrs. Carbonel gave her Mrs. Barnard's letter to read, but the tears came so thick and fast that she could not see it at first, nor indeed fully grasp the meaning, while two pairs of eyes were devouring her countenance as she read. Mrs. Carbonel guessed how it was, and saw that the transports which Dora and Sophy expected were not by any means near, so she gently said, "We will leave you to read the letter, and come again tomorrow to hear what you think."

"Thank you, ma'am; thank you," said poor Judith, as well as she could among her tears.

"How stupid she is!" cried Sophy, as they emerged into the road.

"I don't believe she could read Mrs. Barnard's letter," said Dora.

"No, not for tears," said Mary.

"Do you think she could have understood you?" added Sophy.

"Oh, yes; she understood well enough."

"But how could she be so dull as not to be delighted?" said Sophy.

"So ungrateful, too!" added Dora.

"My dear Dora! It was the embarrassment of her gratitude that touched me so much," exclaimed Mary.

"Do you really think she will not be enchanted to get away from that dismal hole, and live with honest people?" asked Sophy.

"My dears, I think you have quite forgotten that Mrs. Dan Hewlett is her sister."

"Nobody would think so," said Dora.

"If she could only take Johnnie and Judy away with her," said Sophy, "before their father has spoiled them."

"You can't think she would refuse such an offer!" added

Dora. "To be with a good, nice woman, and at peace among her friends. It really would be quite wicked in her to refuse."

Nevertheless, Mary withstood all the entreaties of her sisters to go with her to hear Judith's decision. Edmund heard them persuading her, and in his peremptory manner desired them to desist. So they hovered about the garden and home-field waiting for news.

But the news was not what they expected. Mrs. Carbonel found Judith very tearful, but resolute.

"I could not do it, ma'am! I am sorry, sorry to the heart, to seem ungrateful for her kindness; but, indeed, I could not do it. I cannot leave my sister and the children."

"You would be so much more comfortable — so much better looked after."

"Yes, ma'am, I know that. Mrs. Gregg is one of the best of women, and so kind. It is very good of her to be willing to take me in; but — "

"You need not be afraid of the journey. Mrs. Barnard will come for you."

"Oh yes, ma'am, I know; but there's my sister, ma'am, and her children. I could not leave them."

"I was afraid they did not know how to take care of you, and that your brother-in-law was rough with you."

"My sister have been much better of late, since you have been here, ma'am; and the poor children, ma'am, I can do something for them."

"I see that John and Judy seem to respond to your care; but is it right to give up all your comfort and peace, and even your health, for so little as you are enabled to do for them? It would be better if there were some appreciation of your care, or some attention paid —"

"Molly is generally good to me. Yes, she is, ma'am; and poor little Johnnie, there ain't nothing he would not do for me. I'm greatly obliged to Mrs. Barnard and the dear young ladies. I would dearly like to see them again; but Molly is my sister, and my sister is my sister, and I can't feel it right to leave her."

"I honour you, Judith. It is a right feeling. But when they neglect you, and prey upon you, can it be incumbent on you to give up all for their sakes?"

"I don't know, ma'am; but my poor sister, she has a hard life, and I think her husband would be worse to her if I went away. I couldn't have no comfort in thinking of them if I did."

"Do they know of this? Have they been persuading you?"

"No, ma'am; I did not say a word. Molly was out, and I wanted to think it out without being worried and terrified."

"Quite right, Judith. I am glad they do not know," said Mary, who had learned that "terrified" did not mean frightened, but "tormented." "I can well believe you have decided in true unselfishness, and in the fear of God. But if you see reason to change your mind, let me know in the course of the week."

Dora and Sophy were really quite angry at Judith's refusal, especially Dora, who had taken all the trouble of representing her condition to the Barnards.

"I should call it ungrateful," she said, "only I believe it is pure weakness and folly. Those people have been bullying her and tormenting her out of consenting."

"You are wrong, Dora," said her sister, "they know nothing about it! This is all her own doing."

"And," said Edmund, "if you were older, Dora, you would know how to appreciate a very noble act of self-denial."

Dora did not at all like Edmund to talk of her being older; but what he had said gave her something to think about, and she began to reverence the feeling that made Judith Grey choose the rough and ungenial life with the Hewletts, to comfort and sympathy with her friends.

Mrs. Carbonel and Judith were mistaken in thinking the transaction could pass unknown to the rest of the family. Polly was near at hand, but had hidden herself, on the lad's approach, for fear of being called to account for not being at school, and she reported to her mother that "Madam Gobbleall had been ever so long with aunt, a-trying to persuade her to go away, and live with them fine folks as she was in service with."

Molly had a certain real affection for her sister; but to both her and Dan, the removal would be like the loss of the goose that laid the golden eggs, and there is no saying what poor Judith had to go through. Molly came and cried torrents of tears, taking it for granted that Judith meant to go, and must be frightened out of it. It was of no use to declare that she had refused the lady. Molly was so much in the habit of semi-deception, that she could not believe the assurance; and to hear her lamentations over her dear sister, for whom no one could do like a blood-relation, and her horror at the idea of strangers being preferred to herself, one would have thought — as indeed she believed herself — that she was Judith's most devoted and indefatigable nurse. And to think of them Gobble-alls being so sly, such snakes in the grass, as to try to get her away, unknownst! She would not have them prying about her house again.

Dan declared it was all the cunning of them, for fear Judith should become chargeable to the parish, and there! her fine friends would die, or give her up, or she would just be thrown on the parish, and passed on to a strange workhouse, and then she would see what she got by leaving her kin. It was just like their sly tricks!

In point of fact, if Judith had become chargeable to the parish, Dan's remarks would have been equally true of Uphill, whence she would have been handed to the place where her father had lived, and it was the object of every place to dispose of all superfluous paupers. But Dan and Molly wished her to imagine them willing to keep her freely, in case of a failure of the supplies!

Poor thing! They really thought that their opposition had induced her to drop the idea, and that it was for their own ease, or the good of the rates, that the Carbonel ladies had tried to persuade her to leave them. Molly did not forbid the ladies the house — there was too much to be made out of the pickings from their presents — so Judith did not lose the cheerfulness and comfort they brought her; but Dan laid up the proposal in his mind as another cause of hatred and ill-will to Captain Carbonel.

CHAPTER XV.

Scales of Justice.

"Thou hast appointed justices of peace to call poor men
before them for matters they were not able to answer."
— *Shakespeare.*

When the Parable of the Wheat and the Tares was spoken,
the Blessed and only Wise foresaw the extreme difficulty of
rooting out the tares without injuring the wheat, when the
work is done by the ignorant or hasty hands of the servants.

So it was at Uphill. Captain Carbonel was made a county
magistrate, and thus had more power in his hands, and his
most earnest wish and prayer was to use it for the good of the
parish. But things were very difficult. At the vestry, the farmers agreed with him that Barton and Morris ought not to have
additional parish relief, great strong men as they were, who
had both refused extra hours of labour offered by farmers, of a
kind they did not like, and now demanded help on the score of
their large families. In fact, it had become the custom to
demand relief for every fresh child that was born, and the men
were often idle in consequence. There were men with many
children who had never come on the parish, because they were
trustworthy and sober, and their wives were thrifty. Each
magistrate could point to several of these, and each knew how
the small and struggling ratepayers were oppressed. Nor could
it be fair that these men should be maintained in idleness or
dawdling at the expense of the hard-working small shop-
keepers.

Every gentleman on the bench who had weakly yielded
before, and had given an order to whoever tramped over to ask
for it, was very glad to have some one who would speak out,
and take the burthen of unpopularity. So the order was not
given, and Barton and Morris walked home disappointed, but
not till they had each taken a pint or two of beer at the "Blue
Lion" on their way home, uttering many curses on "that there

Gobbleall." Captain Carbonel did not hear those same curses, but as he rode home he saw the two men stagger out of the "Blue Lion," refreshed not only by their own pints, but by those of sympathisers. And the sight did not make him sorry for what he had done, knowing well that George Hewlett, Cox the cobbler, and Mrs. Holly, the widow with a small shop, were almost borne down with the rates, and not seeing why they should toil that Billy and Nanny Barton should lounge and drink.

Billy Barton, however, did more. He joined an expedition which Dan Hewlett was already organising with Joe Todd, as much for revenge as profit, to have a night of poaching in Mr. Selby's woods, in which there were a number of fine pheasants, not so many as at present where preserves are strictly kept, but poaching was more profitable in some ways, since in those days poulterers were not allowed to sell game openly, but gave a higher price to men who could contrive to convey it to them, and then sold it at a great profit to pretentious people, who had no friends to give it to them, but who wanted to show it at their dinner-parties. Tirzah Todd, as usual, was the means of disposing of most of these gains. Her lively ways made poulterers and servants inclined to further her dealings.

She was a great deal too sharp to carry any save her lawful wares to Greenhow Farm; but in the last year since the Carbonels had come, especially since the captain had been a magistrate, the trade had been less prosperous and required more caution. Once Captain Carbonel had found a wire for a hare in his hedge, and had made it known that he should prosecute any one whom he caught out. He was no eager sportsman himself, but he had a respect for the law.

The poachers arranged a raid upon the Selby woods, in which Joe Todd, Dan Hewlett, and Billy Barton all took part. The first of these was too sharp to be caught by the keepers. He had all the litheness and cunning of his gipsy blood, and was actually safe in the branches of a tree overhead, while Dan, having put his foot into a rabbit-hole, was seized by one keeper, with his gun and a bag of spoil, and Billy Barton, in his bewilderment, ran straight into the arms of another, with a pheasant's tail poking up his short smock-frock as it stuck out of his pocket.

Of course Mr. Selby could not commit for an offence against himself, so Hewlett and Barton were hauled off to Captain Carbonel, while their wives begged to see madam, and they were conducted to the verandah, for the justice business was going on in the large kitchen. No doubt they expected, though Nanny had read no novels, that the magistrate would sit enthroned in the most public place in the house, that the women would weep, that the ladies, with softened hearts, would throw themselves before him, like Queen Philippa at Calais, and beg off the victims. Of what could, should, or ought to be done, they had no notion; and of course they were both in terrible distress, Nanny crying passionately into her apron, and protesting — whenever she could get voice between her sobs, that if the good lady would get the good gentleman to forgive him this time — he would never, never do so no more. While Molly Hewlett, who had some remnants of old respectability about her, was trying her utmost to induce Mrs. Carbonel to intercede.

It was the first time. He was led to it. It was for sport. He had never done it before. To be sure madam would not let 'em be hard on poor Judith's brother. No Hewlett — no, nor any Grey — had ever been in prison before! He was just drove to it, because that there George would give him no work! She and her poor children would have to come to the workhouse, and poor Judith! Nanny, too, began to cry out about her poor children and the parish.

Meanwhile Mrs. Carbonel had been trying to get in a word to make them understand that the matter did not rest with the captain, and that he had no choice at all in the question but to commit them to gaol to take their trial. He had no power to let them off, and she could do nothing, though she was sincerely sorry for the wives; but they neither heard nor tried to hear, and as the cart was driven up by Master Pucklechurch, the keeper, and the constable Cox, to the back door for the handcuffed prisoners, weeping and wailing of the loudest arose, and the women darted round to embrace their husbands, evidently expecting Mrs. Carbonel to assure them that she would charge herself with the support of their families while they were in prison.

She was so much distressed, and so pitiful, that she was just going to do something of the kind, but her husband's gesture stopped her. Billy Barton howled more loudly than his wife, and, as he could not raise his hands to his face, presented a terrible spectacle, though the captain declared there were no tears to be seen. Dan stood grim, stolid, and impassive, and if he spoke at all, it was in a muttered oath at the noise his wife was making. It was a great relief when the cart was driven off, followed by the two women, and Captain Carbonel exclaimed —

"Poor creatures! That Barton is a fool, but Mr. Dan is something worse."

"Oh, those poor women! Why would you not let me speak, Edmund, and promise that they should not starve?"

"The parish will take care of that, Mary; you need not be afraid."

"It sounds so hard-hearted," said Dora and Sophy to each other.

But Edmund did not prevent, nor wish to prevent, their going to see Judith, nor taking with them much more solid food than she was in the habit of eating. Thick sandwiches and lumps of cold pudding were likewise conveyed to the Barton children at school, so that probably they fared much better than was their usual habit.

Judith said she was sorry that Dan should go for to do such a thing, but she was less indignant than Dora expected, and she cried, though more quietly than her sister, when he was sentenced to three months' imprisonment. It was to be said for Molly Hewlett, that enough of her old training remained about her to keep her a sober woman, but Captain Carbonel saw Nanny Barton reeling out of the "Blue Lion" on the day of the conviction, much the worse for the treatings she had enjoyed by way of consolation.

If George Hewlett had any strong feelings about his brother's disaster, he did not communicate them; he went about his work just as usual, and whistled as much as ever. But he took Johnnie, who was only eleven years old, into his workshop, and gave him eighteenpence a week for doing what he could; and he turned out handy, diligent, and trustworthy, so as to be fully worth the money, and thus to stay on when his father came out of prison.

Dan was much the same man as when he went into gaol, save that his hatred to Captain Carbonel had increased.

CHAPTER XVI.

Linch-Pins.

"And leave them laughing, Ho! Ho Ho!"
— *Robin Goodfellow.*

Notice was sent from the Bishop of the diocese that he was about to hold a Confirmation at Poppleby in six weeks' time. This was matter of rejoicing to Mr. Harford, who had mourned over the very few communicants. Before he came the Celebrations had been only three times a year, and were attended by most of the aged paupers. To the joy of the Carbonels, the feast was monthly after his coming; but the first time the aged people were there, and all lingered, George Hewlett, the clerk, said, when the curate looked to him for information —

"The alms, sir. They be waiting for the money in the plate."

"Why, that is to be reserved for sick and distressed."

"Mr. Selby, he always give it out to them, and so did Mr. Jones afore him, sir. They be all expecting of it."

Mr. Harford thought that it might be best not to disappoint the old people suddenly, so he stood at the vestry door counting heads, and numbering among them two whom he had already been somewhat startled to see present themselves, namely, Dame Spurrell, whom he had heard abusing her neighbour with a torrent of foul words, and who pretended to be a witch, and Tom Jarrold, whom Hewlett had described to him as the wickedest old chap in the parish.

He took counsel with the churchwardens, Farmers Goodenough and Rawson, who both agreed that they were a bad lot, who didn't deserve nothing, but it helped to keep down the rates. Then he talked to Captain Carbonel, who, being a reverent man, was dismayed at what he heard.

"Just paying the old souls for coming in no fit state," he said.

"Then you advise me to change the system?"

"You have no other choice," returned the soldier. "Read out

your standing orders, and preach, if you will, explaining the matter."

This Mr. Harford did, but not by any means all the persons concerned were present, and he afterwards went round among them explaining that, though they were to be helped in any distress, and the alms would be kept for the purpose, it was profane to give them out as a sort of payment to those who partook. Old Redford, Widow Mole's father, was the only person who seemed to enter into the scruples.

"Yes, sir," he said, "it went agin me to sim to be paid for coming to the Lord's Table, and I wouldn't ne'er ha' done it, but a shilling is a shilling to my poor daughter, and when I could get to church, it was hard on her to miss the chance."

The next Celebration was only attended by the Carbonels, old Mrs. Rawson, and Redford; nor at the next ensuing Whitsuntide were the numbers much increased. In spite of all that Mr. Harford could preach, and say in private, the main body of the parishioners would not listen to the invitation. And the disaffected grumbled among themselves, that he kept the money for himself, and no one would never see the colour of it. There really were only thirteen communicants in the parish when these had seceded. And Mr. Harford looked to the Confirmation to bring more intelligent and devout worshippers, though the time for preparation was short.

He found that most people had been confirmed at Minsterham Cathedral, and there were reminiscences of great holidays, few and far between, and no difficulty was made as to the young people, up to twenty years old, being nominated for Confirmation. There was some disappointment that it should be only at Poppleby, as furnishing so much less of a day's pleasure; and when it was found that Mr. Harford expected the candidates at regular classes and private lectures, there were objections. Farm lads could not be spared, maids in farmhouses still less.

"What should parson want to be always at 'em," said Mrs. Goodenough. "Old Mr. Jones, he never made no work with them."

However, she had two daughters to be confirmed, and the

reigning "Lizzie" was allowed to go as an escort to them. The elder lads, who were really grown men, would not come at all, and could never be found. "They wouldn't be catechiz — not they." The Sunday scholars, male and female, came pretty well, but not in large numbers, and the age fixed for Confirmation was fifteen, so that those who were fresh from teaching were not many. Sophia Carbonel was a candidate, and very much in earnest, but Mr. Harford preferred giving her books to read and questions to answer in private, as with most of the others he had to begin at the very beginning. The Misses Goodenough knew almost nothing — far less than Susan Pucklechurch and Rachel Mole, who were the gems of the female class, as was Johnnie Hewlett of that of the youths. The brightest of these was, however, in some respects, Fred Allen, of the general shop. He had been at school at Downhill, and could really read and write better than Johnnie, and far better than any one else; for the chief scholars only made what Betty Pucklechurch called "a sad hackering job of un," and most scarcely knew a letter, having forgotten whatever they might have learnt at Dame Verdon's before they went out bird-starving. Fred Allen began by answering, when asked what was done in Confirmation, "Taking all your godfather's and godmother's sins upon you, and becoming liable to be balloted for the militia!" It was a startling view, and, as far as Mr. Harford could make out, it was shared by most of the candidates; but, then, they had very little notion of what sin meant, as, if they had a general idea, it was plain that they did not seriously expect to suffer for their sponsors sins after Confirmation, or that the sponsors suffered for theirs previously.

The curate taught, questioned, explained, and exhorted. Fred Allen knew little, but his wits were sharper, and he took in Mr. Harford's instructions more readily, and remembered them better, while apparently most of the other minds were, and remained, a blank. Only he could not refrain from causing horse-laughs outside, and making grins at every opportunity.

But, with much anxiety, and after many exhortations, Mr. Harford gave out his tickets. The girls were to be conveyed — the most of them — in the Greenhow waggon, driven by old

Pucklechurch, the boys to walk. Mr. Goodenough would drive his daughters; and Sophia, in her white dress and cap (nobody wore a veil then), would be with her sisters and brother in the chariot with post-horses. Captain Carbonel and Mr. Harford went outside on the box.

They had passed Downhill, and were getting on, as well as their horses could, through the muddy ground at the bottom, freshly stirred up by a previous wet day. Before them was a steep, short ascent, but at the bottom of this there was a sudden stop. The captain put his head in at the window and said, "Only the cart — no harm," and strode on following Mr. Harford, while the ladies craned their heads out, and Dora, exclaiming "An accident," ran after him, and Mary only just withheld Sophy, in consideration of her white dress, on the post-boy's assurance, with a scarcely suppressed grin, "No harm done, ma'am. Only they lads."

For what the two gentlemen and the amused post-boy had seen was this. The squadron of boys had overtaken the cart full of girls, when, just as the waggon had come to the pitch of the hill, all the load of maidens were seen tumbling out at the back, and as the horses of the chariot halted, the girls' screams, mingled with the horse-laughter of the boys, was plainly to be heard. Only Susan Pucklechurch, sitting on the front seat with her father, remained in her place. The girls were giggling and helping one another up, nearly all unhurt, but some very angry, and Bessy Linwood was scolding violently, Pucklechurch likewise in his most growling voice, "Ye young good-for-noughts! I'll lay the cart whip about your idle, mischievous backs," while the party of boys were still laughing, and one voice was heard to shout, "Rubbish shot here." A peal of laughter followed, but was cut short by Bessy Linwood's, "Here's parson; you'll catch it." Then, at the top of her voice, "Sir, 'tis them boys! They've bin and pulled out the linchpins and shot us all down into the mud!"

"Is this so?" said the captain sternly, while silence came down on the party, except for the sobs of Jenny Hewlett, who had gone into a dirty pool, and whom Rachel Mole and Betsy Seddon were brushing down vigorously.

"Quite true, sir," returned Pucklechurch. "They young dogs got behind, and played the poor maids this trick."

"Who did?" demanded Mr. Harford.

Bessy Linwood spoke up and said it was "all on 'em," but she saw Fred Allen at it.

No doubt, the fun of the thing had been too much for the boys, in their holiday mood of thoughtlessness, and they stood looking sheepish, but Mr. Harford was very stern and sharp with them.

"Lads, do you think that, if you could play such a trick, you can be in a fit state to take solemn vows upon you?"

No one spoke up except Fred Allen. "We didn't do 'em no harm," he said.

"No harm! To disturb all good thoughts in their minds and your own, and drive out all serious impressions by this mischievous trick! Now, will any one come forward and say he is sorry?"

Mr. Harford waited, but no one stirred. He bade the girls get in again, and Pucklechurch drive them on. He waited again, but no one spoke. Indeed, Allen and another big youth were seen making for a gap in the hedge.

"Will no one say he is sorry for what was an idle trick, but very wrong when you ought to be thinking how you would be giving yourselves up to God?"

They stood like stocks, and Captain Carbonel said, "Has no one the grace to regret a very improper and thoughtless action?"

Still no one moved.

"Then," said the clergyman, "there is no choice left to me. It would be profanation to take persons in such a mood to make vows, and kneel to receive God's grace, which they evidently make light of. Whoever will not come and apologise must go home."

There was no movement among the white round frocks. Boys are like sheep: what one does, the others do, and few are to be found to stand alone. Mr. Harford looked anxiously at Johnnie Hewlett and one or two more, from whom he expected better things, but they only looked down, with their hands in their pockets and sullen faces; and Captain Carbonel held up his watch to show that they should all be too late. There was nothing to be done but to return to their seats, and urge the post-boy to hurry on.

The bells of Poppleby church might ring merrily, but the heart of the curate was very heavy with the questions — whether this misfortune could be owing to his not having impressed the lads enough while preparing them, or to his having been too hasty and peremptory in his indignation.

Captain Carbonel said they were such intolerable louts that to disappoint them was all the better, and they would know how to present themselves more seriously another time, but Mr. Harford much doubted whether they would ever present themselves again.

"It would just be mockery for them to make the vow," said the captain.

"Ah! they miss the grace," said the curate.

Harriet Allen was crying all through the time of the Confirmation when she perceived that her brother's head was not among the boys. Indeed the only male candidate from Uphill was Will Cox, who had gone with his cousins from Downhill. Most of the boys were glad to have got off making the vow, for, in spite of all Mr. Harford's teaching, there were some who still believed that they would take all their god-parents' sins upon them, or, at any rate, that they should feel more bound to take heed to their ways.

Johnnie Hewlett indeed was sorry when he went home to his aunt, and had to tell her why he had not been confirmed after all.

"Oh, Johnnie, Johnnie, you didn't go for to upset the maids?"

"I? No. I was at the bottom of the hill with Harry Coles."

"Then why couldn't you have said so?" He hung his head and twisted his hands. "Oh, Johnnie, what was it? Was it only the going along with the others?"

Still he made no reply, but Judith saw in his face that this was the reason.

"Oh, my boy! To think that you did not feel that God's

blessing and grace were worth standing out for against a lot of idle chaps; and now you won't be able to take the Sacrament!"

"Father never would let I," returned the boy.

"Oh, my dear, dear lad, don't you know that you might have got strength, and would get strength, to stand up for yourself, and do what you ought. Oh dear! My hope is gone!" she cried bitterly, and though Johnnie got away from the sight, her distress really found its way into his heart, while he said very little except, "There, there, auntie, never mind. Maybe I'll try again next time."

"You promise me, John Hewlett; even if I'm not here to see?"

"Yes, I promise, aunt," said he, glad to have silenced her regrets, and hoping the fulfilment was a good way off.

The parishioners, especially those who had only sons and not daughters, were very angry. They did not value Confirmation greatly, but that the curate after "making such a work with the poor lads as never was," should have presumed to reject them made them furious. Mr. Allen even threatened to write to Dr. Fogram, but as he did not know how to address a letter to what he called "Oxford College," he contented himself with walking off with his belongings to Downhill church every Sunday — that is, when they went anywhere.

CHAPTER XVII.

Progress or no Progress.

"For some cry quick and some cry slow,
But while the hills remain,
Uphill, too slow, will need the whip,
Downhill, too quick, the chain."

Tennyson.

Several years had passed away, and Mary's Approach had never been made, though the lane had been improved and worn a good deal smoother, and the Duchess and other grandees had found their way along it.

There were other expenses and other interests. Dora was married. A fellow-soldier of Captain Carbonel's had come on a visit, and had carried the bright young sister off to Malta. She was a terrible loss to all the parish, and it would have been worse if Sophia had not grown up to take her place, and to be the great helper in the school and parish, as well as the storyteller and playmate, the ever ready "Aunt Sophy" of the little children.

And these years had made the farm and garden look much prettier and neater altogether. The garden was full of flowers, and roses climbed up the verandah; and the home-field beyond looked quite parklike with iron railings between, so that the pretty gentle Alderney cows could be plainly seen.

The skim-milk afforded by those same cows went in great part to the delicate children in the village, though Mrs. Carbonel had every year to fight a battle for it with Master Pucklechurch and his wife, who considered the whole of it as the right of the calves and little pigs, and would hardly allow that the little human Bartons or Morrises were more worth rearing.

There had been a visitation of measles through the village — very bad in the cottages, and at Greenhow the three little children had all been very ill; the second, Dora, died, and the elder one, little Mary, remained exceedingly delicate, screaming herself ill on any alarm or agitation, and needing the most anxious care.

The cottagers had learnt to look to Greenhow and the "Gobblealls" as the safe resource in time of any distress, whether of a child having eaten too many blackberries, or of a man being helpless from "rhumatiz;" a girl needing a recommendation to a service, or "Please, sir, I wants to know if it is allowed for a man to kill my father?" which was the startling preface to George Truman's complaint of a public-house row in which his father had got a black eye.

Still, there was less fighting among the men and much less among the women, since Nanny Barton and Betsy Seddon had lodged counter-accusations after a great quarrel over the well, when Nanny had called Betsy, among other choice epithets, "a sneaking hypercriting old cat of a goody," and Betsy had returned the compliment by terming Nanny "a drunken, trapesing, good-for-nothing jade, as had no call to good water." On which Nanny had torn out a large bunch of Betsy's hair, and Betsy had used her claws to make long scratches on Nanny's cheeks, the scars of which were cherished for the magistrates! It was expected in the village that Betsy would get off, being that she and her husband worked for Captain Gobbleall, and Nanny was known, when "a bit overtaken," to have sauced Miss Sophy. Nevertheless they were equally fined, with the choice of three weeks' imprisonment, and, to every one's surprise, the fines were produced.

Betsy thought it very hard that she should be fined when she worked in the captain's fields; and she lamented still more when he insisted on the family removing to a vacant cottage of his own between two of his fields. It was in better condition, had more garden, and a lower rent, and her husband, who was a quiet man, never quarrelling unless she made him, much rejoiced. "She have too much tongue," he said, and she had to keep the peace, for the captain declared that, after the next uproar in his fields, he should give her no more work there. And though she declared it was not her, but "they women who would not let her alone," things certainly became much quieter.

For Captain Carbonel was an active magistrate, busy in all the county improvements, and preserving as much order in the two parishes as was possible where there was no rural police, only the constable, Cobbler Cox, who was said to be more "skeered of the rogues than the rogues was of he," and, at Downhill, Appleton, the thatcher, who was generally to be found enjoying himself at the Selby Arms. Still, fewer cases came up to the bench than in former times, and Uphill hardly furnished one conviction in a quarter. The doctors at the infirmary said that they knew an Uphill person by the tidier clothing. This was chiefly owing to the weekly club, of which the women were very glad. "It is just as if it was given," they said, when the clothes came in half-yearly, and decent garments encouraged more attendance at church. There was no doubt that Uphill was more orderly, but who could tell what was the amount of real improvement in the people's hearts and souls?

That first Confirmation had only produced two additional communicants, Sophia Carbonel, and Susan Pucklechurch, who was in training in the Greenhow nursery. Not one of the others came to the Holy Feast. Their parents, for the most part, said they were too young, and, as these parents never came themselves, the matter seemed hopeless unless some deeper religious feeling could be infused by diligent care.

In one case, where there was a terrible illness and a slow recovery of George Truman, he became strongly impressed, and so did his wife, a very nice, meek woman, who had been in a good service. They both came to the Holy Communion the month after the man was out again, but he did not keep it up. "Sir, if you knew what the talk was like out in the fields, you would not wish it," he said. Which gave Mr. Harford much to think about.

The next Confirmation, three years later, collected nearly the same number of boys and girls, and Mr. Harford walked with the boys himself, and sent Mrs. Thorpe with the girls, so that there was no such scandal as before. The only lad who presented himself from among those rejected of the former year, was Johnnie Hewlett. He was by this time older than any of the other candidates, and he had learnt in a measure to stand alone, though it was chiefly his promise to his aunt that brought him now. He still worked with his cousin George Hewlett, and was a good deal trusted, and made useful. His father had, however, drifted farther and farther away, since George had absolutely refused to employ him again in his business.

"You never know where you are with such as he," said George, and with good reason; but Dan laid it all to "they Gobblealls and their spite." It was so far true that it was the depredations at Greenhow Farm that first convinced George that Dan was an absolute pilferer, though he had before suspected it, and tried to shut his eyes to the doubt. Dan, being a really clever workman, far brighter-witted than George, had lived upon chance jobs at Downhill or Poppleby, together with a good deal of underhand poaching, which he kept as much as possible from the knowledge of his family, never being sure what Molly might not tell her sister, nor what Judith might disclose to the ladies. Polly had made a miserable marriage, and Jenny was in service at a public-house, Jem, a big idle lad, whom no one employed if it could be helped, Judy was still at home, and a comfort to her aunt.

It was his aunt that chiefly induced John to live at home, though he could easily have lodged away and have been nearer to the workshop. His father had let him alone, and not interfered with his Sunday School going, as long as he was a mere boy, till this second time, when, at eighteen, and grown to man's stature, he was going up as a candidate with the younger ones. Then the father swore "he was not going to have his son make a tomfool of hisself to please that there parson."

"I have promised," said John.

"Promised? What — parson or ladies, or any sneaks that come meddling where no one wants 'em?"

"'Twere not parson," said John.

"Then 'twas one of they Gobblealls" — with an oath. "That ain't of no account."

"'Tweren't," again said John.

No more was to be got out of him than "'Tweren't," and "I shall keep my word." He was too big to be beaten; a tall, strong, well-made youth, and Dan was obliged to let him alone, and only swear at him for turning his back on his old father, and being no better than a Methody.

In point of fact, Molly and the two younger children were chiefly supported by John's earnings and Judith's pension, for whatever Dan earned at Downhill or picked up in his various fashions was pretty sure to be swallowed either by the "Blue Lion" or by the "Fox and Hounds." Judith was entirely in bed upstairs, and the kitchen had lost all the little semblance of smartness it once had. While Molly might have been taken for sixty years old instead of forty-five, though that was not unusual among the hard-working women, who got aged and dried up with weather in the fields and with toil and care at home — even when they had kindly, sober husbands.

Judith's room was a place of peace and order, so kept by the help of little Judy and of John, both of whom loved her heartily, and felt as if she were a mother to them. She had brought home to them all the good that they knew. She had always made them say their prayers by her as children, and John continued to do so still, "for old sake's sake if for no other reason." They had always repeated to her what they had heard at school, and by-and-by the text and substance of the sermons as far as they could; and she told them her own thoughts, freely and earnestly, thoughts that came partly from the readings of Mrs. Carbonel and Mr. Harford with her, but far more than she knew from her own study of the Bible, backed by her earnest spiritual mind, which grew deeper and deeper as her earthly sufferings increased. Of course she had tried to do the same with her sister and the other children, but none of them would endure it. Molly always had something to do elsewhere, and said what was all very well for a sick woman like Judith could not be expected in one who had such a lot of trouble that she did not know which way to look.

Poor thing! Neither Judith nor Mr. Harford could persuade her that there was a way to look which would have lightened all these troubles! But John had learnt how to stand alone, and he did so, not only by presenting himself for confirmation, but by becoming a Communicant. Not another lad did so, but his cousin George and his wife had begun at last, under the influence of Mr. Harford's sermons, and so had a few more in the parish. John, in his cousin's workshop, was shielded from a good deal of the evil talk and jesting that went on among his fellows in the fields. He "took after" George in being grave and quiet, and he loved no company better than his invalid aunt's; but to be a steady and religious youth was a more difficult matter in those days than at present, for harmless outlets for youthful spirits had not been devised, and to avoid mischief it was almost needful to abstain from almost all the company and pleasures of a country lad.

CHAPTER XVIII.

The Threshing-Machine.

"When lawless mobs insult the court,
That man shall be my toast,
If breaking windows be the sport,
Who bravely breaks the most."
Cowper.

Captain Carbonel had made his farming answer better than his friends, or still more the farmers, had predicted. He had gone to the markets and talked with the farmers, and not shown off any airs, though, as they said, he was a gentleman, so known by his honest, straightforward dealing. Nor had he been tempted to launch out into experiments and improvements beyond what he could properly afford, though he kept everything in good order, and used new methods according to the soil of his farm.

Master Pucklechurch growled at first, and foretold that nothing would come of "thicken a'"; that the "mangled weazel," as he called the mangel wurzel, would not grow; and that the cows would never eat "that there red clover as they calls apollyon;" but when the mangel swelled into splendid crimson root and the cows throve upon the bright fields of trifolium, he was as proud as any one, and he showed off the sleek sides of the kine, and the big mis-shapen roots of the beet with the utmost satisfaction.

Equal grumbling heralded the introduction of a threshing-machine, which Captain Carbonel purchased after long consideration. The beat of the flail on barn floors was a regular winter sound at Uphill, as in all the country round, but to get all the corn threshed and winnowed by a curious revolving fan with four canvas sails, was a troublesome affair, making farmers behindhand in coming to the market. And as soon as he could afford the venture the Captain obtained a machine to be worked by horse-power, for steam had hardly been brought as yet into use even for sea traffic, and the first railway was only opened late in 1830, the time of the accession of William the Fourth.

The farm people, with old Pucklechurch at their head, looked at the operations of the machine with some distrust, but this gradually became wonder and admiration on the part of the Greenhow labourers, for threshing with the flail was very hard work for the shoulders and back, and Captain Carbonel took care to find employment for the men in winter time, so that his men did not join in the complaint of Barton and Morris that there wouldn't be nothing for a poor chap to get his bread by in the winter. In truth, the machine and its work were a perfect show to the neighbourhood for the first harvest or two, when Seddon was to be seen sitting aloft enthroned over a mist of dust, driving the horse that went round and round, turning the flails that beat out corn from the ears in the sheaves with which Pucklechurch and Truman fed the interior.

All Greenhow was proud of its "Mr. Machy," as the little Mary called it, thinking perhaps that it was a wonderful live creature.

The neighbourhood remained quiet even when George the Fourth died, and there was much hope and rejoicing over the accession of his brother, who was reported to be the friend of the people, and to mean to make changes in their favour. Poor old George Hewlett was, however, much exercised on the first Sunday, when, in the prayers for the king, Mr. Harford inadvertently said George instead of William, and George Hewlett, the clerk, held it to be praying for the dead, which he supposed to be an act forbidden.

There was, of course, an election for the new parliament, but it did not greatly affect Uphill, as nobody had any votes, except Captain Carbonel, the farmers, and the landlord of the "Fox and Hounds," and the place was too far from Minsterham for any one to share in the election news, except Dan Hewlett and Joe Todd, who tramped over thither to hear the speeches, swell the riotous multitude, and partake of all the beer to which both sides freely treated all comers. They came home full of news, and reported in the bar of the "Fox and Hounds" that there were to be grand doings in this new parliament; the people wasn't going to stand it no longer, not if the right gentlemen got in; but there would be an end of they machines, as made horses do men's work, and take the bread from their poor children. Beer would be ever so much cheaper, and every poor man would have a fat pig in his sty. That is, if Mr. Bramdean, as was the people's friend, got in.

"Why, he was the one as our Captain Gobbleall was agin," observed Cox, who had come in to hear the news.

"To be sure he was; Gobbleall is hand and glove with all the tyrums. Ha'n't he got a machine?" said Dan, in an oracular manner.

"No one will never tell me as how our captain ain't a friend o' the people," returned Seddon. "Don't he get coals reasonable for us, and didn't he head the petition for your pig, Jim, and draw it up, too?"

"Ay, but what right had he to say my missus shouldn't take it out of the parish?" said Jim Parsons. "We'd a made a couple of pounds more, if she'd been free to go her rounds, as Betty Blake did."

"Ay, that's the way of 'em. They grudges us everything what they don't give themselves," said Dan, "and little of that, too."

No one understood the spirit which desired to make people independent, and raise them above indiscriminate beggary, and Todd said, with a grim laugh, "They would not see us make a little purse for ourselves, not if they can help it."

Seddon feebly said the ladies was free enough with their gifts. "They had never had no one before to help the women folk and the children."

"Pig's wash! Much good may it do 'em," said Dan, so contemptuously that Seddon durst not utter another word in the general laugh, though he carried home a little can of milk every day, and he and others well knew the store that their wives set by the assistance of their little ones.

They knew it well enough, though they were afraid to maintain the cause of the Gobblealls before such an orator as Dan; and nothing worse than these grumblings took place all harvest time, where the whole families were fully employed, the men each taking a portion of the field, while their wives and children aided in the reaping and binding, and earned sums amongst them which would pay the quarter's rent, buy the pig, and provide huge boots for the father, if for no others of the family. The farmers provided substantial luncheons and suppers for the toilers in the field; and, when all was over, and the last load carried, amid joyful shouts, there was a great harvest supper at each farm, where songs were sung, dances were danced, and there was often a most unlimited quantity of beer swallowed.

No one had then thought of harvest thanksgivings; but at Greenhow there was as usual the farm supper, but with only ale enough for good and not for harm; the ladies came to hear the songs in the great farm kitchen, and the party had to break up at nine o'clock. The women, especially Mrs. Mole, were glad; but the men, even the steady ones, did not like having only half an evening of it, and "such a mean sup of beer." It really was excellent strong beer — far better than the farmers' brew — but that did not matter to the discontented, who, instead of letting themselves be taken home by their wives, adjourned to the "Fox and Hounds," and there sat over their pint cups, replenished from time to time, while they discussed the captain's meanness, and listened to a dirty old newspaper, which told of the doings of Jack Swing, who was going about in Wiltshire, raising mobs, threatening farmers and squires, and destroying machines. There was much excitement among the gentry about Reform, but apparently the poor cared not about it.

To the Uphill mind, Wiltshire was as strange and distant a country as Australia, and this made little impression, so that, as the days went on, everybody went to their usual work, and there was no alarm.

"Oh no," said Mrs. Carbonel, "the people here have far too much good sense to want to molest their best friends. They quite admire our threshing-machine; and see what a saving of labour it is!"

However, it was thought right to raise a body of yeomanry

for the defence of the country, in case the disaffection should become more serious, and the assistance of Captain Carbonel at the county town was urgently requested to organise the members of it. He left home for a few days without the least anxiety. And Mr. Harford, too, went on the Monday to attend a college meeting at Oxford, and would not return till he had visited his patient lady-love. The Selbys were away, spending the autumn at Cheltenham.

CHAPTER XIX.

A Night Journey.

"And he must post, without delay,
Along the bridge and through the dale.
And by the church and o'er the down."
Wordsworth.

John Hewlett had finished his day's work, and come home in the dusk of an October evening. He found the house hung all over with the family linen, taken in to shelter from a shower; but not before it had become damp enough to need to be put by the fire before it could be ironed or folded. His mother was moaning over it, and there was no place to sit down. He did not wonder that Jem had taken his hunch of bread and gone away with it, nor that his father was not at home; but he took off his boots at the back door, as his aunt never liked his coming into her room in them — though they were nothing to what he would have worn had he worked in the fields — and then climbed up the stairs.

Judith was sitting up in bed, with her teapot, tea-cup, and a piece of stale loaf, laid out on a tray before her; and little Judy beside her, drinking out of a cracked mug. Judith's eyes had a strange look of fright in them, but there was an air of relief when she saw Johnnie.

"Well, aunt, is that all you have got for tea?"

"Poor mother has been hindered; but never mind that," returned Judith, in a quick, agitated tone. "Judy, my dear, drink up your tea and run down to help mother, there's a dear."

"You haven't brought nothing, Johnnie," Judy lingered to ask.

"No, not I. I've worked too late to go to shop," said Johnnie.

"Go down, my dear, as I told you," said Judith, with a little unwonted tone of impatience, which made the youth certain that she had something important to tell him; and as soon as the little girl began clumping down the stairs, she held out her hand and said in the lowest of voices, "Come near, Johnnie, that you may hear." He came near; she put out her hand to pull him on his knees, so that his ear might be close to her, and whispered, "Jack Swing is coming to Greenhow tomorrow."

"The captain away! How do you know?"

"A man came and talked with your father in the back garden — just under this window. Mother had run up to shop for a bit of soap; but they thought she might come in any minute, and so went out at the back door, so that I heard them all the better."

"They never thought of that! Well?"

"They mean to come on Greenhow, ask for money and arms, break up the machine, and burn the ricks if they don't get what they want. Father said they might be sure of the Downhill men, and most of 'em here, for they all hate that there machine that is to starve poor folk in winter time; and those that were not of that way would be afraid to hold back, or they would show them the reason why."

"And the captain away. It is enough to be the death of madam and the little ones."

"That's just what I thought. Oh, Johnnie dear, can't you help to save them, and hinder it?"

"Master wouldn't go along with such doings," said John.

"I wouldn't answer for George! He's a steady man, and would do no harm if he's let alone; but he's a mortal fearsome one! No, John, there's no help for it, but that you should get over in time to fetch the captain, and let him take away the ladies, or stand up for them. He'll know what to be at!"

"But will it get father into trouble?" asked John.

"Not among so many. He's sharp enough. The captain, if he were only at home, would see how to get them away. Anyway, think of the poor ladies and the little children!"

John stood for a minute or two by the window thinking, while Judith sat up in her bed gazing at him with eager, anxious eyes; and at last he turned back, and would have spoken aloud but that she raised her hand to caution him. He knelt down again beside her, and said, "No, aunt, I couldn't rest to think of all those rough brutes of chaps from we don't know where coming and playing their rigs, and bullying the ladies, with no one to help. There was a lady frightened to death with them, — master was reading it out in the paper. Yes, I'll go and fetch the captain home to take care of them. Where is he?"

"Miss Sophy told me he was at the hotel at Minsterham with a lot of them. Have you ever been there, Johnnie?"

"Yes. Once I went with master in the cart when he wanted a bit of mahogany wood for Mrs. Goodenough's chairs. It is a long way," said Johnnie, looking wistfully at the darkening window; "but I'll do it, please God."

"Yes. Please God, and He will help you. You've had your tea. No! Well, drink up this, — it is cold enough — and take this hunch of bread. I am afraid there's nothing better to be had. And here's sixpence, in case you want a bit of food."

"I've got ninepence of my own," said John, feeling in his pocket; and though most of his pay went to his mother for his washing and board, he always kept a little back every week.

"There, then, you'd best be off, my dear lad. Keep out of sight, you know, as long as you are in the village."

Johnnie bobbed his head; and his aunt threw her arms round his neck, and kissed him, as she had not done since he was in petticoats; and then she murmured, "God bless you, my darling lad, and take care of you."

Johnnie did not feel the prayer needless, for in spite of his eighteen year, he had all a country lad's dislike of being out alone in the dark; and to this was added the sense that it was a time when evil-minded people might be about, who would certainly assault and stop him if they guessed his errand. To meet his father would make it certain that he would be seized, abused, beaten, and turned back, with the reproach of being an unnatural son — turning against his father. Of this, however, there was little chance, as Dan Hewlett was pretty certain to be either in the "Fox and Hounds" or in the "Blue Lion" collecting partisans. And Johnnie, getting out through the back door, then by the untidy garden, and over the wall of the empty pig-stye, cut out into a stubble field. He was not afraid of his mother missing him till bedtime, as it was the wont of the youths — especially of those who had comfortless homes — to wander about in parties in the evening, bat-fowling some-times, but often in an aimless sort of way, doing little bits of mischief, and seeking diversion, which they seldom found, unless there was any solitary figure to be shouted at and star-tled. His father was not likely to come in till after he was turned out of the public-house; so John strode, all unseen, across the field, and through the gateway into the next. He did think of the possibilities of bringing arrest and prosecution upon his father; but this did not greatly trouble him, for at this early period no regular measures of defence had been taken against the rioters; and as they went about disguised, and did not, as a rule, threaten life, they generally escaped scot-free.

And the idea of a rude mob terrifying Mrs. Carbonel to death was terrible to him. Even since the day when she had stood before him in the Sunday School at the wash-house at Greenhow, she had been his notion of all that was lovely and angelic in womanhood. She had said many a kind word to him over his work, and little Miss Mary had come and watched him with intense interest, eager chatter, and many questions when he was mending the gate.

He was obliged to go down to the bridge at Downhill so as to cross the river, but there were lights in the houses, and a sound of singing in the "Blue Lion," which made him get into the fields behind as soon as possible, though by this time it was quite dark, so that he had to guide himself as well as he could by the lights in the windows. This led to a great many wander-ings and stumbles, since he did not know every field with its gates and gaps as well as he knew Uphill, so that he lost a good deal of time by blundering about, looking for a lighter space in the hedge which might or might not lead into the next field. He made his way up to the opening. It proved to be a gap, but lately mended, and he ran a couple of thorns deep into his hand before he tumbled over into a ditch.

This was a grass field, and he heard the coughings of an old sheep, and the suppressed baaings of the others, finding himself presently outside their fold. He guided himself along by the hurdles and came to deep ruts in stiff clay, but these led to a gate, and that into a narrow and muddy lane. This he knew would bring him back to the high road, and that was comparatively plain sailing.

Still there was Poppleby to go through, though not for several miles, which he tramped along, quietly enough, not meeting any one, but beginning to hear the sounds of the night-loving animals.

Owls flew about with their hootings and snappings, startling him a good deal, as much from some notions of bad luck as from wonder at first if it were a human shout. Then the lights of Poppleby were welcome to his eyes, and as they were chiefly in the upper windows he thought the town must be safe to walk through without fear of being met and stopped. Gas-lamps hardly existed then and Poppleby was all dark except for the big lamps over the public-house doors, and this was well for Johnnie, for just as he was about to pass the "Blue Lion," the door was thrown open, and a whole party came swaggering and staggering out, singing at the tops of their voices. Johnnie had time to throw himself into a garden behind a hedge, and heard them pass by, holloaing rather than singing out —

> "Down, down with they machines
> That takes the poor folks' bread."

There was something too about "Friends to the people and foes beware"; but what startled Johnny the most was that he knew his father's voice in the shout, and for one moment saw the light of a lantern fall across a face that could belong to no one else but his father. It could hardly be told whether, as he lay trembling there, the sight made him the more dislike his expedition, or the sound of those cries the more anxious to bring protection to his friends at Greenhow. Anyway, he had given his word to his aunt, and he must go through with it, and he fancied that he could get to Minsterham before the keepers of late hours were shut up for the night, and might return again to see how things were going, and get excused by his cousin.

Not till the shouts had died away in the distance did he venture out, and plodded once more into the darkness, under overhanging trees, meeting nothing, except one carriage, whose bright lamps came on like two fiery eyes, glowing more and more as they came nearer, and the black shadow of horses, driver, and close carriage rushed by, and left him again, deciding that it must be the doctor's chariot. Then came another long long spell, so long that he thought it must be near morning, and was surprised to hear behind him in the frosty air the church clock at Poppleby striking far too many strokes, and what he hoped had been one turned into either eleven or twelve! He hoped it was twelve.

There were the branching roads, and it was far too dark to read the sign-post, so that he could only take the one that seemed to him the most likely; but when he had gone what might be any distance on the road, it seemed to get narrower and rougher than he expected, and then came an opening as if on to a common, such as he was sure did not exist on the way to Minsterham. He must have got upon the Elchester road, and there was nothing for it but to turn back. However, there was a pale brightness showing in the sky, and the moon came up, an old moon without very much light in her, but she was a great comfort to him, and told him how the night was going.

On and on, and then there was a sound of trampling of horses and of wheels coming nearer, great light eyes growing larger and larger, and the mail-coach flashed and thundered by with the four horses, and presently, far-away he could hear the guard's horn announcing the approach to a wayside inn where the horses were changed; but by the time Johnnie had made his weary way up to the place, it was far-away on the road, indeed, he saw the lamps flash as it went up Wearyfoot Hill, but all the inn was silent again by that time even at the stables, and the hotel was a dark mass against the sky — the only light in it the moon reflected from the windows. A dog barked as he went past, but he kept far upon the other side of the road and was reassured by hearing the rattling of a chain.

Wearyfoot Hill! Yes, it was Wearyfoot to him, as he dragged up it. He could not remember whether it was four or five miles from Minsterham. There was a milestone standing on the bank, and he tried to read it, but the moon would not reveal more than the large initial letters of L for London and M for Minsterham, and he sat down at last and leaned against the stone, trying to trace out the figure above Minsterham with his fingers.

Behold, though four and five were both ringing in his head, he must have fallen asleep, for he felt quite cold and stiff, the moon was much higher in the sky, the stars were paler, and there was a mist all round. He rose up, ashamed, and shook himself, colder and more uncomfortable than before, but feeling it was a new day, and that, were it four miles or five, he was now near Minsterham. He said his morning prayers as he tramped along, stamping to warm his feet, and recollected that Aunt Judith would be lying awake praying for him. He found that when the first discomfort of awakening had passed off, he really was the better for his short sleep, and marched on more vigorously, presently hearing a cock begin to crow, and birds to twitter. Dawn was beginning, presently a lark sprang up and began to send down a wonderful cheerful song, that quite raised Johnnie's spirits; then over the quiet misty fields came the deep note of the great Minsterham clock pealing out, what was only a half hour, but John knew that it would be much louder in his ears next time it spoke.

A waggon lumbered by, and then a labourer or two going to their work, but John kept out of their way, not wanting to be asked questions; there began to be red in the eastern mist, the clock sounded again, and from the slope of the hill, the spires of the churches in the town seemed to be rising out of a great lake of woolly mist. The clock went through all the four quarters, then solemnly told out five strokes — Johnnie's weary night journey was over.

CHAPTER XX.

The Royal Hotel.

"O haste to aid, ere aid be vain."

Scott.

Though Johnnie's journey was over, his troubles were not at an end. When he came to the first houses, the way seemed still to lengthen out before him, and everything appeared to be still asleep, though the daylight was coming in as brightly as a foggy morning allowed. Nor did he know his way; he had only driven to a timber-yard once with his cousin, and dined with him at a little public-house close by, and had no more than a dim recollection of shops, which looked quite different now, with all their shutters up. Only a milk-cart, coming in with full tins, seemed to give a sign that people would want their breakfast some time or other; and next appeared a very black sweep with his cart, and two miserable little bare-footed boys running beside it, as black as the silhouette over Mrs. Thorpe's chimney.

Half-past five struck, and charwomen began to come out of side alleys, baker's shops to take down their shutters. Johnnie ventured to ask one of the apprentice boys doing so the way to the Royal George Hotel.

"D'ye want to bespeak the best apartments?" was all the answer he got, as the lad stopped his whistling and looked superciliously at Johnnie's battered, dusty working dress, and old straw hat.

He found he should only be laughed at and walked on, renewing his question when he saw a good-natured-looking woman in a black bonnet and stout canvas apron, apparently going out for a day's washing.

"Is it the Royal or the King George Tavern as you mean, my son?" she asked him.

"Oh! the Royal — the one where the gentlemen goes," said Johnnie. "I've got a message for one of 'em."

"Bless you, my lad, they won't never let you in at this time of morning," said the woman.

"It's very particular," returned John. "I came off at night to tell him."

She looked at him curiously. "And what might it be, young man! Some one taken very bad, no doubt."

"No — not that," said John, and she looked so kind, he could not help telling. "But he have got a machine, and Jack Swing is coming, and if he don't come home to see to the poor ladies —"

"Bless me, and who may it be?"

"Captain Carbonel — out at Uphill."

"Never heard tell of the place."

"It's out beyond Poppleby."

"My! And you've comed all that way tonight?"

"The ladies are very good. He's a right good gentleman. All one to the poor as to the rich."

"I say! You are a good young man, to be sure! I'd go with you and get to the speech of Lavinia Bull, the chambermaid, what I know right well; but if I'm not at Mrs. Hurd's by six o'clock, she'll be flying at me like a wild cat. Mercy on me, there it goes six! Well, if that fine dandy, Boots, as is puffed up like a peacock, won't heed you, ask for Lavinia Bull, and say Mrs. Callendar sent you, and he will call her fast enough."

John thanked her and was going off at once, but she called out, "Bless the boy, he's off without even hearing where to go! Just opposite the City Cross, as they calls it."

It was not much like a cross to Johnnie's mind, being a sort of tower, all arches and pinnacles and mouldered statues, getting smaller up to the spiring top; but he knew it, and saw the hotel opposite with all its blinds down, nothing like astir yet, except that some one was about under the great open doorway leading into a yard, half entrance, to the hotel.

He could see a man brushing a shoe, and went up with "Please, sir —" But he was met by, "Get off you young vagabond, we want none of your sort here."

"Please, sir, I have a message for Miss Bull;" he hesitated.

"She ain't down. Get off, I say. We don't have no idle lads

here."

"It's very particular — from Mrs. Callendar."

"Old witch! Have she been burning any one's shirt fronts. I say, Jem, you see if Lavinia is in the kitchen, and tell her old Callendar has been burning holes in her stockings or collars, and has sent a young scarecrow to tell her."

John opened his mouth to say it was no such thing; but the under shoeblack, who was a sort of slave to Boots, made an ugly face at him, and was gone, turning coach wheels across the yard. In another minute Lavinia, a nice brisk looking young woman, had come up with, "Well, young man, what has Mrs. Callendar been after now?"

"Please, ma'am, nothing; but she said as how I was to ask for you. It's for Captain Carbonel, ma'am, a message from Uphill — that's his home."

"Captain Carbonel — that's Number Seven," she said, consulting a slate that hung near the bar. "He was to be called at eight o'clock. Won't that do?"

"Oh no, no, ma'am," implored John, thinking that the captain was taking his rest away from home. "It's very particular, and I have come all night with it."

"You have got to call Number Five for the High Flier at half-past six," she said, turning to Boots. "Could not you take up word at the same time?"

"Catch me running errands for a jackanapes like that," said Boots, with a contemptuous shrug, turning away, and brushing at his shoe.

"Never mind him," said good-natured Lavinia. "What shall I say, young man?"

"Oh, thank you, miss. Say that John Hewlett have brought him a message from Uphill."

"Jack Owlet! Oh my! Hoo! hoo!" exclaimed the blacking boy, as soon as Lavinia had disappeared up the stairs, dancing about with his hands on his hips. "Look here, Tom," — to a boy with a pail, who had just come in — "here be an Owlet's just flown in out of the mud. Hoo! hoo! Where did you get that 'ere patch on your back."

"Where you never got none," responded the other boy.

"Mother stitched it for him."

"Ay, sitting under a hedge, with her pot hung up on three sticks and a hedgepig in it," added the younger Boots. "Come, own up, young gipsy! Yer come to get a tanner out of Number Seven with your tales."

"I'm no gipsy," growled John; "but — "

"Come, come," called out Boots, "none of your row. And you, you impudent tramp, don't ye be larking about here, making the lads idle. Get out of the yard with ye, or I call the master to you."

The landlord might probably have been far more civil; but poor Johnnie did not know this, and could only move off to the entrance of the court, so that when Lavinia in another moment appeared and asked where he was, Boots answered —

"How should I tell? He was up to mischief with the boys, and I bade him be off."

"Well, Number Seven is ever so much put about, and he said he would be down in a jiffy! So there!"

Lavinia held up her skirts, and began in her white stockings to pick her way across the yard, while Boots sneered, and began brushing his shoe, and whistling as if quite undisturbed; and in another moment Captain Carbonel did appear, coming down the stairs very fast, all unshaven, and with a few clothes hastily thrown on, and quite ran after Lavinia, passing her as she pointed out beyond the entrance, where John was disconsolately leaning against the wall with his hands in his pockets, feeling how utterly weary and hungry he was, and with uneasy thoughts about his father coming over him.

"Oh, there you are, John Hewlett! What is it? No one ill?" exclaimed the captain.

"No, sir; but," — coming nearer and lowering his voice — "Jack Swing, sir."

"Jack Swing! We had notice of him out at Delafield."

John shook his head, and looked down.

"What! Do you know anything, my boy? Here, come in — tell me!"

"Please, sir, they've laid it out to come to Greenhow this very day as is, to break the machine and get the guns and money."

The captain started, as well he might; but still demanded, "How do you know?"

John held his head down, most unwilling to answer.

"Look here, my lad, you've done well coming to warn me; but I must be certain of your news before acting on it. We were to ride off to Delafield today, and I must know if this is only a rumour."

"Aunt heard them," said John, between his teeth. "She heard them planning it for tomorrow — that's today — and she laid it on me to let you know to save the ladies from being fraught."

"Your aunt heard it?"

"Through the window in the back garden. They planned to get all the chaps at Downhill and all, and go at the machine."

"The villains! Who did? No, I'll not ask that, my lad," said the captain, knowing only too well who it must have been; "you have acted nobly, and I am for ever obliged to you. Come in, and have some breakfast, while I dress and report this, and see what is to be done. You are sure there is time?"

"They was to go about at dinner-time to get the folks," John squeezed out of his mouth, much against his will.

"Then there's time. Thank you with all my heart, John! I'll see you again. Here," — to a barmaid who had appeared on the scene — "give this young man a hearty good breakfast and a cup of ale — will you? — and I'll be down again presently. Stay till I come, Hewlett, and I'll see you again, and how you are to get home! Why, it is twenty miles! Were you walking all night?"

"Only I went to sleep a bit of the time when I was trying to make out the milestone; I don't rightly know how long it was," said John, so much ashamed of his nap that the captain laughed, and said —

"Never mind, Johnnie, you are here in the very nick of time; eat your breakfast, and I'll see you again."

The good-natured barmaid let John have a wash at the pump with a bit of yellow soap and the round towel, and he was able to eat his breakfast with a will — a corner of cold pie and a glass of strong ale, such a breakfast as he had never seen, though it was only the leavings of yesterday's luncheon. Everybody was too busy just then to pay him any attention, and he had time to hear all the noises and bells seem to run into one dull sound, and to be nodding in his chair before he was called by a waiter, with — "Ha, youngster, there, look alive! the gentlemen wants you."

Now that sleep had once begun upon him, assisted by the ale, John looked some degrees less alive, though far more respectable than on his first arrival. He was ushered into the coffee-room, where three or four gentlemen sat at one table, all in blue and silver, with the captain, and as he pulled his forelock and bobbed his head, the elder of them — a dignified looking man with grey hair and whiskers and a silver-laced uniform, said — "So, my lad, you are come to warn Captain Carbonel of an intended attack on his property?"

"Yes, sir," John mumbled, looking more and more of a lout, for he had thought the captain would just go home alone to defend his wife and his machine, and was dismayed at finding the matter taken up in this way, dreading lest he should have brought every one into trouble and be viewed as an informer.

"What evidence have you of such intentions?"

John looked into his hat and shuffled on his foot, and Captain Carbonel, who knew that Sir Harry Hartman, the old gentleman, was persuaded that Delafield was the place to protect, was in an agony lest John should be too awkward and too anxious to shield his family to convince him. He ventured to translate the words into "How do you know?"

His voice somehow made John feel that he must speak, and he said, "Aunt heard it."

"What's that? Who is aunt?" said Sir Harry, in a tone as if deciding that it was gossip; but this put John rather more on his mettle, and he said, "My aunt, Judith Grey, sir."

"How did she hear?"

"Through the window. She heard them laying it out."

"She is bedridden," put in the captain; "but a clever, sensible woman."

"Whom did she hear or see?"

"She couldn't see nobody, sir. It was a strange voice," John was trying to save the truth.

"Oh! and what did she hear?"

"They was planning to go round the place and call up the men — that's today," said John.

"Are you sure it was today? Did she tell you she heard it?"

"Yes, sir. And," John bethought him, "there was a great row going on at the 'Fox and Hounds,' and when I came past Poppleby, a whole lot of them come out singing 'Down with the machines.'"

"That's more like it, if it was not a mere drunken uproar," said Sir Harry.

"I suppose you did not know any of the voices?" said one of the other gentlemen.

John could hold his tongue this time. "And you came all this way by night, twenty miles and odd, to warn Captain Carbonel, on your aunt's information?" said Sir Harry, thoughtfully. "Are you sure that she could hear distinctly?"

"One can hear in her room talk in our garden as well as if it was in the room," replied John.

"Well! you are a good lad, well intentioned," said Sir Harry. "Here's half-a-crown to pay your journey back. We will consider what is to be done."

John had rather not have taken the half-crown, but he did not know how to say so, so he pulled his forelock and accepted it.

Captain Carbonel came out of the coffee-room with him, and called to the hostler to let him lie down and rest for a couple of hours, when the Red Rover would change horses there, and then call him, and pay for his journey back to Poppleby.

So John lay down on clean straw and slept, too much tired out to put thoughts together, and unaware of the discussion among the gentlemen. For Sir Harry Hartman was persuaded that it was Delafield that needed protection, and was inclined to make little of John Hewlett's warning, thinking that it rested on the authority of a sick nervous woman, and that there was no distinct evidence but that of the young man who would not speak out, and only went by hearsay.

Captain Carbonel, who was, of course, in an agony to get home and defend his property, but was firmly bound by his notions of discipline, argued that the lad was the son of the most disaffected man in the parish, and that his silence was testimony to the likelihood that his father was consulting with the ringleader. The invalid woman he knew to be sensible and prudent, and most unlikely either to mistake what she heard, or to send her nephew on such a night journey without urgent cause, and he asked permission to go himself, if the troop were wanted elsewhere, to defend his home. Finally, just as the debate was warming between the officers, a farmer came in from Delafield, and assured them that all was quiet there. So the horses were brought out, and there was much jingling of equipments, and Johnnie awoke with a start of dismay. He had never thought of such doings. He had only thought of Captain Carbonel's riding home, never of bringing down what seemed to him a whole army on his father.

Chapter XXI.

Jack Swing.

"Richard of England, thou hast slain Jack Straw,
But thou hast left unquenched the vital spark
That set Jack Straw on fire."
                                    Sir H. Taylor.

Nobody knew who Jack Swing was. Most likely he really
was more than one person, or rather an impersonal being,
worked up as a sort of shadowy puppet to act in the cause of
future reform.

There were hot spirits abroad, who knew that much was
amiss on many points, and who burned to set them right; and
there were others who were simply envious and jealous of all
that had power or authority, and wanted to put these down for
their own profit. They thought that the way to get their cause
attended to was to make the other party afraid of the people,
and they did not know or understand that those who delayed to
grant their wishes only desired patience, and to do the work in
the best and wisest way. All that they demanded, and more
too, has since been given to the people, but gradually, as was
expedient, and without tumult or disturbance.

So there was a desire to frighten the gentry by showing the
strength of the people, in anticipation of the Reform Bill to be
proposed the next year. It would not have made much difference to the country people, for no one would have a vote whose
rent did not amount to ten pounds a year, and they would not
have cared much about it if they had not been told that if it was
passed, every man would have a fat pig in his sty, and be able
to drink his daily quart of beer, moreover, that the noblemen
and gentlemen were resolved on keeping them out of their
rights, making bread dear, and depriving them of their wages
by setting up machines to do all the work.

This last came near home, and stirred up the minds that
would have cared for little else. Just as four hundred years

before, Jack Straw was an imaginary champion whose name inflamed the people to rise, so now Jack Swing, or whoever it was who acted in that name, sent messages round that such and such a place should be attacked at such and such a time.

There was always some one in the town who could be fired with the idea that inciting riot and revolt was patriotism, and that a good cause could be served by evil methods, who cast aside such warnings as "Rebellion is like the sin of witchcraft," or "The powers that be are ordained of God." Besides, the infection spread, and to hear what Jack Swing was doing elsewhere encouraged others not to be behindhand with their neighbours.

So the mandate had gone out, and there were a few at Elchester ready to arrange for a rising at Uphill and Downhill. Dan Hewlett was known to them in the public-house, and he had an especial spite at Captain Carbonel, beginning from his knowledge of the tacit detection of his abstraction of the paper at Greenhow, going through his dismissal from working there, aggravated by the endeavour to remove Judith, embittered by the convictions as a poacher, and, perhaps, brought to a height by the influence over his eldest son. He hated the captain enough to be willing to direct the attack upon Greenhow, especially as it was known that the master was absent and engaged in summoning the yeomanry "to ride down the poor chaps," as it was said, "who only wanted bread for their children's mouths."

There were men both at Uphill and Downhill, and even at Poppleby, who were quite willing to listen. The Poppleby folk, some of them, believed that riot was the only way to get reform, more of the villagers thought it was the only way of getting rid of the machines, the object of mysterious dread for the future, and more still, chiefly ne'er-do-wells and great idle lads, were ready for any mischief that might be going; and full of curiosity and delight at what Jack Swing might be about to do.

These youths, some of them at work and some not, dispersed the news through the village and fields that there was to be a great rising of the people's friends, and that Gobbleall's machine was to be somewhere. All were to meet at the randygo — supposed to mean rendezvous — at the crossroad, and as for those who did not, it would be the worse for them, and worse than all for them that told clacking women who might carry the tale up to Greenhow.

The summons was indeed not given till the men were well out of reach of their clacking women, but at work in the fields, and then a party began — not to march — they could not have done that to save their lives, but to tramp out of Poppleby, shouting to any one whom they saw in the fields to come with them and stand up for the people's rights. At Downhill their numbers increased by all the noisy fellows, and some who fancied great good was to be gained somehow, though some wiser wives called out to them not to get into a row, nor let themselves be drawn into what they would be sorry for. At the "Fox and Hounds" they tarried and demanded a glass of beer all round, which Mr. Oldfellow was really afraid to refuse. He was a timid man, half on their side, half on that of the gentry, and he saw there were enough of them to sack his cellars if he demurred.

There, too, amid much laughter, they all disguised themselves, some blackening their faces with soot, others whitening them with chalk, and some putting on the women's cloaks, bonnets, or aprons.

Then they collected Uphill men.

"We are come for your good," said Jack Swing, or the man who passed for him, wearing a long Punchlike nose. "We are come to help you; and where's the mean coward that won't come along with us in his own cause? There will be no living for poor folks if those newfangled machines be allowed to go on, and them Parliament folk vote out all that makes for the people. Down with them, I say! Up with Reform, and down with all the fools and cowards who won't stand up for themselves."

All this, garnished with foul words and abuse, and roared out from the top of the horse-block, was addressed to the crowd that began to gather.

Dan Hewlett, with a horrid white face, was going about persuading the men, and so were others. "Bless you, we don't want to do no harm to the ladies, nor the children. We only wants to do away with them toady machines, as they wants to do all the work instead of men's hands, as the Almighty meant, and is in Scripture."

This was the plea to the better disposed, like Tom Seddon, who held out, "You'll not hurt madam nor the little ones. She've been a kind lady, and the captain, he's a good master, I will say that; and I don't want to hurt 'em."

"Nobody wants to hurt them; only to do away with they machines."

"I tell you what," was George Truman's answer, "them machines are the captain's, none of yours nor mine, and I won't go for to damage 'em. No! I won't have my face blacked nor whited, I'm an honest man, and not ashamed to show it. So I be going to my work."

And off he went to his day's work at Farmer Goodenough's, and the others hissed him and hooted him, but did him no harm. Nobody made such a noise as Softy Sam, and together this frightened Jem Gibbs out of following him, though he much wished to do so. Will Mole, as soon as he heard any sounds, ran away headlong down towards the meadows, and hid himself in the long rushes. Cox, the constable, thought discretion the better part of valour; and long before the rabble rout appeared, set off to carry a pair of shoes home to Mrs. Pearson at the Lone Farm.

Master Hewlett, the carpenter, looked in vain for John, his apprentice, and growled and grumbled that he did not appear; then, on perceiving the uproar, decided that he was gone after that "there father of his'n." He wouldn't have thought it of Jack. No; he wouldn't; but sure enough it was "bred in the bone of him!" Master Hewlett went on with his planing; and when the troop, now amounting to about thirty grown men, besides a huge rabble of boys and girls, came along, and Dan shouted to him to come and stand up for the rights of the people, and down with that there "tyrum Gobbleall" and his machine to grind down the poor, he answered —

"Machine ain't nothing to me. I minds my own business, and thou beest a fool, Dan, not to mind thine! And where's that lad of thine? A trapesing after mischief, just like all idle fellows?"

"He bain't a labourer, and has no feeling for them as is," said Dan. "We wants your axe, though, George."

"Not he! I dares you to touch him," said George Hewlett in his unmoved way, smoothing off a long curled shaving, which fell on the ground. "There, that's the worth of you all and your Jack Swing! Swing, ye will, Dan, if you don't take the better care."

Some one made a move as if to seize the axe, but George made one step, and lifted quietly the stout bit of timber he had been planing, and it was plain that a whole armoury of carpenter's tools was on his side the bench.

"Come along," said Dan, "he's a coward and mean-spirited cur. Us shan't do nothing with he."

So on they went, all the kindnesses and benefits from Greenhow forgotten, and nothing remembered at the moment but grievances, mostly past, but more looked forward to as possible!

The women did remember. Judith Grey was in an agony, praying as she lay for Mrs. Carbonel and the children. Widow Mole knew nothing, but was weeding the paths at Greenhow; Betsy Seddon and Molly Barnes were crying piteously "at thought of madam and her little girl as might be fraught to death by them there rascals." But no one knew what to do! Some stayed at home, in fear for their husbands, but a good many followed in the wake of the men, to see what would happen, and to come in for a little excitement — whether it were fright, pity, or indignation.

"'Pon my word and honour," said Lizzy Morris, "that there will be summat to talk on."

Chapter XXII.

Great Mary and Little Mary.

"Who'll plough their fields? Who'll do their drudgery for
them? And work like horses to give them the harvest?"
— *Southey.*

Mrs. Carbonel, having seen her two little ones laid down
for their midday nap, was sitting down to write a note to her
husband, while Sophia was gone to give her lesson at the
school, when there came a tap to the drawing-room window,
and looking up she saw Tirzah Todd's brown face and her
finger making signs to her. She felt displeased, and rose up,
saying, "Why, Tirzah, if you want me, you had better come to
the back door!"

"Lady, you must come out this way. 'Tis Jack Swing a-
coming, ma'am — yes, he is — with a whole lot of mischievous
folks, to break the machine and burn the ricks, and what not.
Hush, don't ye hear 'em a hollering atop of the hill? They be
gathering at the 'Fox and Hounds,' and I just couldn't abear
that you and the dear little children should be scared like, and
the captain away. So," as Mrs. Carbonel's lips moved in thanks
and alarm, "if you would come with me, lady, and take the children, and come out this way, through the garden, where you
wouldn't meet none of 'em, I'll take you down the short way to
Farmer Pearson's, or wherever you liked, where you wouldn't
hear nothing till 'tis over."

"Oh, Tirzah! You are very good. A fright would be a most
fearful shock, and might be quite fatal to my little Mary. But
oh, my sister and the servants and the Pucklechurches, I can't
leave them."

"My Hoggie was at home with the baby, and I sent her off
to see Miss Sophy at the school, and tell her to come up to
Pearson's."

"But the Pucklechurches?"

"Nobody will hurt them! Nobody means to hurt you," said

Tirzah, "I knows that! My man wouldn't ha' gone with them, but so as they promised faithful not to lay a finger on you, so you give 'em the money and the guns; but men don't think of the dear little gal as is so nesh, so I thought I'd warn you to have her out of the way. Bless my heart, they'll be coming. That was nigher."

Mrs. Carbonel's mind went through many thoughts in those few moments. She could not bear to desert her husband's property and people in this stress, and yet she knew that to expose her tender little girl to the terrors of a violent mob would be fatal. And she decided on accepting Tirzah's offer of safety and shelter. She ran upstairs, put on her bonnet, took her husband's most essential papers out of his desk and pocketed them, together with some sovereigns and bank-notes, then quietly went into the nursery, where she desired Rachel Mole to put on her bonnet, take up the baby, and follow her, and herself was putting on little Mary's small straw hat and cape, telling her that she was coming with mamma for a walk to see Mrs. Pearson's old turkey cock, when Mrs. Pucklechurch burst in with two or three maids behind her.

"Oh, ma'am, Jack Swing's coming and all the rabble rout. What ever shall we do?" was the gasping, screaming cry.

"Only be quiet. There's nothing for any one to fear. If they do harm, it is to things, not people. I only go away for the sake of this child! No, Mary dear, nobody will hurt you. You are going for a nice early walk with mamma and baby and Rachel. You," — to the maids — "may follow if you will feel safer so, but I do not believe there is any real danger to you. Betty Pucklechurch, please tell your husband that I do beg him not to resist. It would be of no use, his master would not wish it, only if he will take care that the poor cattle and horses come to no harm."

"He have gone to drive 'em off already to Longacre," said Betty. "I tell'd he, he'd better stand by master's goods, but he be a man for his cows, he be."

"Quite right of him," said Mrs. Carbonel. "Have you baby's bottle, Rachel? Now, Mary dear, here's your piece of seed cake."

The shouts and singing sounded alarmingly as if approaching by this time, and little Mary listened and said, "Funny mens singing."

It was very loud as the fugitives gained the verandah, where Tirzah waited with an angry light in her black eyes. "Oh! won't I give it to Joe Todd," she cried, "for turning against the best friend Hoglah ever had — or me either."

Mary, carrying her little Mary, and trying to keep a smile that might reassure her, followed Tirzah across the orchard on the opposite side of the house. They had to scramble through a gap in the hedge; Tirzah went over first, breaking it down further, then the baby was put into her arms, and Rachel came next, receiving Mary from her mother, who was telling her how funny it was to get over poor papa's fence, all among the apple trees, and here was Don jumping after them. Don, the Clumber spaniel, wanted a bit of Mary's cake, and this and her mother's jump down from the hedge and over the ditch, happily distracted her attention, and made her laugh, while the three maids were screaming that here were the rascals, hundreds of them a-coming up the drive; they saw them over the apple trees when on the top of the hedge, and heard their horrid shouts. "Oh, the nasty villains, with black faces and all!"

Mrs. Carbonel dreaded these cries almost as much as the mob itself for her delicate child, and went on talking to her and saying all the nursery rhymes that would come into her head, walking as fast as she could without making her pace felt, though the little maid — albeit small and thin for five years old — was a heavy weight to carry for some distance over a rough stubble field for unaccustomed arms. Tirzah had the baby, who happily was too young to be even disturbed in his noontide sleep, and Rachel Mole had tarried with the other maids, unable to resist her curiosity to see what was doing at the farm since they were out of reach.

The fugitives reached a stile which gave entrance to a rough pathway, through a copse, and it was only here, when her mother sat down on the trunk of a tree taking breath with a sense of safety, that little Mary began to cry and sob. "Oh, we are lost in the wood! Please, please, mamma, get out of it. Let us go home."

"No indeed, Mary, we aren't lost! See, here's the path. We are going to see Mrs. Pearson's pussy cat and her turkey."

"I don't want to. Oh! the wolves will come and eat us up," and she clung round her mother in real terror.

"Wolves! No, indeed! There are no wolves in England, darling, here or anywhere."

"Rachel said the wolves would come if I went in here."

"Then Rachel was very silly. No, there are no wolves. No, Mary, only — see! the little rabbit. Come along, take hold of my hand, we will soon get out. Never mind; God is taking care of us. Come, we will say our hymn as we go on."

The mother said her verse, and Mary tried to follow, in a voice quivering with sobs. Those imaginary wolves were a far greater alarm and trouble to her than the real riot at her father's farm. She clung round her mother's gown, and there was no pacifying her but by taking her up in arms.

"Let me take her, ma'am," said Tirzah Todd, making over the sleeping Edmund to his mother. "Come, little lady, I'll carry you so nice."

"No, no! Go away, ugly woman," cried Mary ungratefully, flapping at her with her hands in terror at the brown face and big black eyes.

"Oh, naughty, naughty Mary," sighed the mother, "when Tirzah is so good, and wants to help you! Don't be a naughty child!"

But the word naughty provoked such a fit of crying that there was nothing for it but for Mrs. Carbonel to pick the child up and struggle on as best she could, soothing her terror at the narrow paths and the unknown way, and the mysterious alarm of the woodlands, as well, perhaps, as the undefined sense of other people's dread and agitation. However, the crying was quiet now, and the sounds of tumult at the farm were stifled by the trees, so that after a time — which seemed terribly long — the party emerged into an open meadow, whence they could see the gate leading to the high road, and beyond that the roof of Mrs. Pearson's house.

But something else was to be seen far up the road. There was the flash of the sun from helmets! The Yeomanry were coming!

"There's papa!" cried Mrs. Carbonel. "Papa in his pretty silver dress. Run on, run on, Mary, and see him."

Mary was let down, still drawing long sobs as she half ran, half toddled on, allowing herself to be pulled by Tirzah Todd's free hand, while her mother sped on to the gate, just in time for the astonished greeting of one of the little troop.

"Mrs. Carbonel! What?"

And the next moment her husband was off his horse and by her side with anxious inquiries.

"Yes, yes, dear Edmund! We are all safe. Good Tirzah came to warn us. Make haste! They are at the farm. We shall be at Mrs. Pearson's. She," (pointing to Tirzah) "sent to fetch Sophy from school. She'll be there. Here are the children all safe."

"Papa, papa," cried little Mary, feeling his silver-laced collar, and stroking his face as he kissed her.

And from that time she was comforted though he had to leave her again at once. She had felt a father's arm.

"Tirzah Todd!" exclaimed Captain Carbonel, "I shall never forget what you have done for us. Never!"

Tirzah curtsied, but said, "You'll be good to my man, sir?"

It was but a moment's halt ere Captain Carbonel rode on to overtake the rest of the troop, who, on hearing that the outrage was really taking place, were riding on rapidly.

Mrs. Carbonel had not far to go before reaching the hospitable farm, where Mrs. Pearson came out to receive her with many a "Dear, dear!" and "Dear heart!" and entreaty that she and the dear children would make themselves at home.

But Sophy was not there, and had not been heard of, and Mrs. Carbonel, in her anxiety, could not rest on the sofa in the parlour, after she had persuaded little Mary into eating her long-delayed dinner of some mutton hastily minced for her, and had seen her safely asleep and cuddling a kitten. Mrs. Pearson was only too happy to have the baby to occupy her long-disused wicker cradle, and Tirzah had rushed off to the scene of action as soon as she had seen the lady safely housed.

Chapter XXIII.

The Machine.

"In bursts of outrage spread your judgment wide,
And to your wrath cry out, 'Be thou our guide.'"
Wordsworth.

Sophy was endeavouring to make the children remember who Joseph was, and thinking them unusually stupid, idle, and talkative, when, without ceremony, the door was banged open, and in tramped Hoglah Todd, with the baby in her arms, her sun-bonnet on her neck, and her black hair sticking wildly out. "Please, ma'am," she began, "Jack Swing is up a-breaking the machine, and mother says you are to go to Farmer Pearson's to be safe out of the way!"

"Hoggie Todd," began Mrs. Thorpe, "that's not the way to come into school," but she could not finish, for voices broke out above the regulation school hush: "Yes, yes, father said," and "Our Jem said," and it ended in "Jack Swing's a-coming to break up the machine." Only one or two said, "Mother said as how it was a shame, and they'd get into trouble."

"Your mother sent you?" said Sophy to Hoglah.

"Yes, ma'am. She's gone up herself to tell madam, and take she to Pearson's, and her said you'd better go there, back ways, or else stay here with governess till 'twas quieted down."

"Hark! They are holloaing."

Strange sounds were in fact to be heard, and the children, losing all sense of discipline, made a rush to snatch hats and bonnets, and poured out in a throng, tumbling over one another, Hoglah among the foremost. Mrs. Thorpe, much terrified, began to clasp her hands and say, "Oh dear! oh dear, the wicked, ungrateful men, that they should do such things. Oh! Miss Sophy, you will stay here, won't you?"

"No, I must go and see after my sister and the children," said Sophy, already at the door.

"But they'll be at Mr. Pearson's. The girl said so. Oh, stay, ma'am! Don't venture. Pray, pray —"

But Sophy had the door open, and with "I can't. Thank you, no, I can't."

There were the confused sounds of howling and singing on the top of the hill. Betsy Seddon, at her cottage door, called out, "Don't go up there, miss; it's no place for the likes of you!" but Sophy only answered, "My sister," and dashed on.

She could get into a field of Edmund's by scrambling over a difficult gate, and, impelled by the sight of some rough-looking men slouching along, she got over it — she hardly knew how — and, after crossing it, came upon all the cows, pigs, and horses, with Pucklechurch presiding over them. He, too, said, "Doan't ye go up there, Miss Sophy. Them mischievous chaps will be after them pigs, fools as they be, so I brought the poor dumb things out of the way of them, and you'd better be shut of it too, miss."

"But, my sister, Master Pucklechurch! I must see to her."

"She'll be safe enow, miss. They don't lift a hand to folks, as I've heard, but I'll do my duty by the beastises."

He certainly seemed more bent on his duty to the "beastises" than that to his wife or his master's wife; and yet, when Sophy proved deaf to all his persuasions, he muttered, "Wilful must to water, and Wilful must drink. But, ah! yon beastises be safe enow, poor dumb things, so I'll e'en go after the maid, to see as her runs into no harm. She be a fine, spirity maid whatsome'er."

So on he plodded, in the rear of Sophy, who, with eager foot, had crossed the sloping home-field, and gained the straw yard, all deserted now except by the fowls. The red game cock was scratching and crowing there, as if the rabble rout were not plainly to be seen straggling along the drive.

Still there was time for Sophy to fly to the house, where, at the door, she met Mrs. Pucklechurch.

"Bless my soul and honour, Miss Sophy. You here! The mistress, she's gone with the children to Mr. Pearson's, and you'll be in time to catch her up if you look sharp enough."

"I shall not run away. Some one ought to try to protect my brother's property."

"Now, don't 'ee, don't 'ee, Miss Sophy. You'll do no good with that lot, and only get hurt yourself."

But Sophy was not to be persuaded. She went manfully out to the gate, and shut it in the face of the disguised men, who came swaggering up towards it.

"What's your business here?" she demanded, in her young, clear voice.

"Come, young woman," said a man in a false nose and a green smock-frock, but whose voice had a town sound in it, and whose legs and feet were those of no rustic, "clear out of the way, or it will be the worse for you!"

"What have you to do here on my brother's ground?" again asked Sophy, standing there in her straw bonnet and pink cotton frock.

"We don't want to do nothing, miss," — and that voice she knew for Dan Hewlett's — "but to have down that newfangled machine as takes away the work from the poor."

"What work of yours did it ever take away, Dan Hewlett?" said she. "Look here! it makes bread cheaper — "

She had thought before of the chain of arguments, but they would not come in the face of the emergency; and besides, she felt that her voice would not carry her words beyond the three or four men who were close to the gate. She might as well have spoken to the raging sea when, as the gate was shaken, she went on with a fresh start, "I call it most cowardly and ungrateful — "

At that moment she was seized from behind by two great brawny arms, and borne backward, struggling helplessly like a lamb in a bear's embrace. She saw that, not only was the gate burst in, but that the throng were pressing in from the garden side, and she was not released until she was set down in Mrs. Pucklechurch's kitchen, and a gruff voice said, rather as if to a little child, "Bide where you be, and no one will go for to hurt you."

It was a huge figure, with a woman's bonnet stuck upright over his chalked face, and a red cloak covering his smock-frock, and he was gone the next moment, while Mrs. Pucklechurch, screaming and sobbing, clutched at Sophy, and held her tight, with, "Now, don't, Miss Sophy, don't ye! Bide still, I say!"

"But, Edmund's machine! His things and all!" gasped Sophy, still struggling.

"Bless you, miss, you can't do nothing with the likes of them, the born rascals; you would, may be, get a stone yourself and what would the master say to that?"

"Oh! what are they doing now?" as a wild hurrah arose, and all sorts of confused noises. Mrs. Pucklechurch had locked the door on her prisoner, but she was equally curious, and anxious for her old man; so, with one accord, they hurried up the stairs together, and looked out at an upper window, whence they could only see a wild crowd of hats, smock-frocks, and women's clothes gathering about a heap where the poor machine used to stand, and whence a cloud of smoke began to rise, followed by a jet of flame, fed no doubt by the quantity of straw and chaff lying about. Sophy and Betty both shrieked and exclaimed, but Betty's mind was chiefly full of her old man, and she saw his straw hat at last. He was standing in front of the verandah, before the front door, and, as they threw the window open, they heard his gruff voice —

"Not I. Be off with you! I baint a-going to give my master's property to a lot of rapscallion thieves and robbers like you, as should know better."

Then came the answer, "We don't want none of his property. Only his guns and his money for the cause of the people." And big sticks were brandished, and the throng thickened.

"Oh, don't ye hurt he!" screamed Betty. "He that never did you no harm! Don't ye! Oh, Dan Hewlett! Oh-oh!"

"Then throw us out the guns, old woman," called up the black-faced figure, "and we'll let him be."

"If you do," shouted Pucklechurch — and then there was a rush in on him, and they could see no more, for he must have backed under the verandah. Betty made a dash for the front stairs, to come to his help, Sophy after her; but, before they could even tumble to the bottom, there was a change in the cries —

"The soldiers! the soldiers! Oh-hoo-hoo-hoo!" There was a scamper and a scurry, a trampling of horses. The two trembling hands, getting in each other's way, unfastened the door, which was not even locked, and beheld Pucklechurch gathering himself up with a bleeding head, a cloud of smoke and flame, and helmets and silver lace glancing through it. There had been no need to read the Riot Act; the enemy were tearing along all ways over the fields, except a few whom the horsemen had intercepted. Dan Hewlett and the black-faced leader, without his long nose, were two; the other three were — among the loudest, poor Softy Sam, who had been yelling wildly — big lads, or young men, one from Downhill, the others nearer home, howling and sobbing and praying to be let go. Captain Carbonel's first thought was whether Pucklechurch was hurt, but the old man was standing up scratching his head, and Betty hovering over him. Then his eyes fell on his sister-in-law, and he exclaimed —

"You here, Sophy! Your sister is very anxious!"

But the fire was by this time getting ahead, and no one could attend to anything else. The prisoners were put into the servants' hall, and locked in; the horses were tied up at a safe distance, the poor things rearing with alarm at the flame; the men were, under Sir Harry Hartman and Captain Carbonel's orders, made to form a line from the pond, and hand on the pails and buckets that were available; but these were not very many, though the numbers of helpers were increased by the maids, who had crept back from the orchard, and by the shepherd and some even of the mob, conscious that they had been only lookers on, and "hadn't done no harm."

It was a dry season, and the flames spread, catching the big barn, and then seeming to fly in great flakes like a devouring winged thing to the Pucklechurches' thatch. Betty and her husband flew to fling out their more valued possessions, and were just in time to save them; but thence the fire, just as the water in the nearest pond was drying up, caught a hold on the dairy and the old thatched part of the farmhouse. Bellowings were heard from the captives that they would be burnt alive, and some one, it was never known who, let them out, for no sign of them appeared when all was over, though their prison was untouched by the fire. For even at that moment the Poppleby fire-engine galloped up the road, and was hailed with shouts of joy. It had a hose long enough to reach down to the brook in the meadow, and the hissing bursts of water poured down did at last check the flames before they had done much harm to the more modern portion of the house, though all the furniture was lying tumbled about in heaps on the lawn — Mary's piano, with the baby's cradle full of crockery on the top of it, and Edmund's writing desk in the middle of a washing stand all upside down.

The first thing Edmund did when the smoke wreaths alone were lingering about, was to send his groom down to the cellar, with a jug in his hand, to bring up some beer, which he proceeded to hand in the best breakfast-cups to all and sundry of the helpers, including Sir Harry Hartman, Sophy helping in the distribution with all her might.

"Miss Carbonel, I think?" said Sir Harry, courteously, as she gave him the cup. "Were you the garrison?"

Sophy laughed. "Yes, sir, except old Pucklechurch and his wife."

"Then I may congratulate you on being the bravest woman in Uphill," said the old gentleman, raising his hat.

It was getting dark, and they had to consider what was next to be done. Captain Carbonel was anxious about his wife and children, and Sir Harry was urging him to bring them to his house, while Mr. Grantley, from Poppleby, who had come up on the alarm, urged the same upon him. It ended in a guard being told off, consisting of Cox, the constable of Uphill, who had emerged from no one knew where, the Downhill constable, and the shepherd, with one of the yeomen, who were to be entertained by Pucklechurch and the cook, and prevent any mischief being done to the scattered furniture before morning. The Pucklechurches and Mrs. Mole, with Barton, were doing their best to bring in and attend to the live stock, all of which had been saved by Pucklechurch's care.

Then they rode off together, Sophy and the housemaid having already started across the fields, bearing whatever necessary baggage they could collect or carry for Mrs. Carbonel and the little ones.

Mrs. Carbonel was at the door when her husband rode up, having only just managed to hush off her little Mary to sleep, and left her and the baby with Rachel Mole to watch over them. Poor thing, she had been in a terrible state of anxiety and terror for all these hours, so much the worse because of the need of keeping her little girl from being agitated by seeing her alarm or hearing the cries, exclamations, and fragments of news that Mrs. Pearson and her daughters were rushing about with.

When she saw him first, and Sophy a moment afterwards, she sprang up to him as he dismounted, and greeted him with a burst of sobs and thankful tears.

"Why, Mary, Mary, what's this? One would think I had been in a general engagement. You, a soldier's wife! No; nobody's a hair the worse! Here is Sir Harry Hartman wondering at you."

To hear of the presence of a stranger startled Mrs. Carbonel into recovering herself, with "I beg your pardon," and her pretty courtesy, with the tears still on her face; while the old gentleman kindly spoke of the grievous afternoon she had had, and all the time Mr. and Mrs. Pearson were entreating him to do them the honour to come in and drink a glass of wine — for cake and wine were then considered to be the thing to offer guests in a farmhouse.

Sir Harry, aware of what farmhouse port was apt to be, begged for a glass of home-brewed ale instead, but came in readily, hoping to persuade Mrs. Carbonel to send for the Poppleby post-chaise, and let him take her and her children home. She was afraid, however, to disturb little Mary, and Mrs. Pearson reckoned on housing them for the night, besides which his park was too far-off. So it was settled that Sophy, for whom there really was no room, should go to Poppleby Parsonage with Mr. Grantley for the night, and she and Sir Harry only tarried to talk over the matter, and come to an understanding of the whole as far as might be.

"Who warned you?" asked the captain.

"The last person I should expect — Tirzah Todd, good woman," said Mrs. Carbonel. "She came and called me, and helped me over the hedges."

"And Hoglah came after me," said Sophy, "and told me to come here, only I could not."

"You were the heroine of the whole, Miss Carbonel," said Sir Harry.

"Oh, don't say so; I didn't do any good at all," said Sophy, becoming much ashamed of her attempt at haranguing. "Old Pucklechurch was the one, for he saved all the dear cows and horses, and was nearly letting himself be killed in the defence. But, oh! all the rest of them. To think of them treating us so after everything!"

"Most likely they were compelled," said gentle Mrs. Carbonel.

"They will hear of it again," said Sir Harry. "Could you identify them, Miss Carbonel?"

"A good many," said Sophy, "though they had their faces chalked — that horrid Dan Hewlett for one."

"There can be no doubt of him, for he was one of the prisoners that got away," said Captain Carbonel, in a repressive manner. "He has always been a mischievous fellow; but the remarkable thing is that it was his son who came to summon us this morning — John Hewlett, a very good, steady lad. By-the-by, has any one seen him? I sent him home by the Elchester coach. I wonder what has become of him."

Chapter XXIV.

Misjudged.

"That weary deserts we may tread,
A dreary labyrinth may thread,
Through dark ways underground be led."
Archbishop Trench.

Poor Johnnie was not very happy at that moment. He had descended from the coach at Poppleby, and set out to walk to Downhill, wondering how he should be received at his cousin's workshop. Everything seemed strangely quiet as he crossed the fields, where he had wandered last night, but there were now and then far-off echoes of voices and shouts. He avoided the village of Downhill, and made his way towards the little street and common of Uphill, but not a creature could he see except Todd's donkey and a few geese.

The workshop was shut up, no one was about either there or at the house. He considered a moment whether to try to see what was doing at Greenhow, or to go and tell his aunt how he had fared, and that he knew the captain must be at home by this time.

He was glad he had decided on the latter, for the cottage door stood open, and Judith was sitting up in bed, her eyes wide open, and her breath panting with anxiety and terror.

"Oh, Johnnie, my dear! There you are! Oh, they are all gone! The ladies, the dear ladies, and the little babies," she gasped, and fell back almost fainting.

"The captain is there by this time, and the soldiers, never you fear," said John. "Here, you'd better take this," trying to drop out some of the cordial he knew she took in her attacks.

"The soldiers! Your father — your poor father!" she gasped again, and she was so ill that John, dreadfully frightened, could only hold her up on one arm, and press the cordial to her lips with the other hand. It was an overdose, but that hardly mattered; and before very long, just as she was beginning to quiet down, there approached a fresh sound of screaming, and his mother burst into the house. "Oh, my poor man! My poor Dan!" she cried. "They have got him! The soldiers have got him!" and, as John was laying down his aunt to come and hear, she rushed up the stairs with, "And it is all your doing, you unnatural, good-for-nothing varmint! That was what you were after all night, you and your aunt, the adder that I have warmed at my bosom! Turning against your own poor father, to set them bloody-minded soldiers on him! And now he'll be taken and hanged, and I shall be a poor miserable widow woman all along of you!"

This was poured forth as fast as the words would come out of Molly's mouth, but before they had all streamed forth, Judith was choking in a hysterical fit, so like a convulsion that Johnnie could only cry, "Aunt! aunt! Mother, look!" And Molly herself was frightened, and began to say, "There! there!" while she helped him to hold her sister, and little Judy flew off, half in terror and half in search of help, crying out that aunt was in a fit.

Help of a certain sort came — a good deal more of it than was wanted — and the room was crowded up, and there were a good many "Poor dears!" "There, nows!" and proposals of burnt feathers and vinegar; but Mrs. Spurrell, who was reckoned the most skilled in illness, came at last, put the others out, especially as they wanted to see about their husbands' teas, and brought a sort of quiet, in which Judith lay exhausted, but shuddering now and then, and Molly sobbed by the fire. John gathered from the exclamations that the Carbonel family were safe somewhere, that Miss Sophy had gone on like the woman preacher at Downhill, that Greenhow had been on fire, but nobody was hurt, though the soldiers had ridden in upon them, "so as was a shame to see," and had got poor Dan and Ned Fell, and all sure locked up.

John was shocked at this, for he had not meant to do more than send Captain Carbonel home to protect his family, and had not realised all the consequences. In a few minutes more, however, his father himself tramped in, and the first thing he did was to fall on the lad in a fury, grasping him by the collar, with horrible abuse of him for an unnatural informer, turning against his own father, and dealing a storm of heavy blows on him with a great stick. Down clattered Mrs. Spurrell, asking if he wished to kill his sister-in-law?

"A good thing too — a traitor in one's house," he burst out, with more raging words and fresh blows on poor John, who never cried out through all; but his mother rushed down the next moment, crying out that she would not have her son mauled and beaten, and laying fast hold of the stick.

It was turning into a fight between husband and wife, and Mrs. Spurrell, who had more of her senses about her than any one else, called out, "Off with you, John Hewlett! I'll tackle 'em!"

Poor Johnnie had no choice but to obey her. Bruised, worn out, hungry, uncertain of everything, and miserable about his aunt, he could only wander slowly away, feeling himself a traitor. He found his way to the workshop, and had just thrown himself down in the wood-shed, when he heard his master's voice calling out —

"Who's there?"

"Me! Johnny! Father's in a mortal rage with me for telling the captain, but I never thought as how all the soldiers would come."

"And a very good thing they did, to put a stop to such doings as never was," said Mrs. Hewlett's voice. "Bless me, the dear children and the ladies might have been burnt in their beds!"

"Come in, Johnnie, and have a bit of supper," said George Hewlett.

"And tell us all about it," said his wife. "We'll give you a shakedown for the night if you can't go home."

John was thankful, and Mrs. Hewlett set before him a good meal of bread, cheese, cold bacon, and beer; but he was too dull and dejected, as well as much too tired, to be able to talk, and scarcely could remember all that had happened. He knew it was not manners to put his head down on his arms on the table, but he really could not hold it up, and he had dozed off almost with the food in his mouth.

"Poor chap! He's fair worn out," said the elder George. "Make his bed ready, mother."

And when it was ready, the younger George absolutely kicked him into being awake enough to tumble into it. Even then his sleep was for a good while tossing, dreamy, and restless; but, by-and-by, it grew sounder, and he lay so still in the morning that his kind hostess hindered her boys from disturbing him. He had not long been awake, and had only said his prayers, and washed at the pump, when horses' feet were heard, and Cousin George called to him to come out and speak to the captain. He came, with hair wringing wet, and shy, awkward looks.

"My lad," said the captain, "I cannot tell you how much I thank you for your bravery and spirit the night before last. You did me and mine a benefit that I shall always remember, though I feel it would just be insulting you to offer you any present reward! Nor, indeed, could it be sufficient for what you have done."

"Thank you, sir," mumbled John, hardly knowing what he or the captain said.

"And," added Captain Carbonel, "your father got away. If he is taken, what you have done for us may be remembered in his favour."

Again John managed to say, "Thank you, sir." And the captain rode off to offer the like thanks to Tirzah Todd; but her cottage was shut up, the donkey gone, and she, with her husband and Hoglah out on a broom-selling expedition. He was not clear of the riot, and she did not want him to hear her thanked. They must have gone away with their gipsy kin, for they never came back while the Carbonels were in England, and only a sovereign could be left for them with Mr. Harford, who promised to stand Tirzah's friend if any opening for assisting her offered.

Dan had been told that rioters generally got off without difficulty. It was not easy to trace them, and their safety was in numbers and their semi-disguise; and Jack Swing, or the man with the nose, had escaped on various similar occasions, wearing a different disguise at each place. It had not come into their calculations that they had gone so far as to rouse the spirit of the landowners, who had at first dealt gently with the disturbances, but who now felt that strong measures must be taken to prevent the mischief from going further. He thought himself safe when he had once got away from the strong-room at Greenhow, and he was slouching about his garden when Cox the constable, backed by two stout men, came with a warrant, from Sir Harry Hartman, for the apprehension of Daniel Hewlett for peace-breaking and arson. He began to argue that it was not he more than any one else, and he hadn't set fire to nothing, but he was told that he must reserve his defence for his trial, and the handcuffs were put on, and he was carried off in a cart, just as John was hurrying up the lane, having got leave from his master to see how his aunt was, before beginning work.

Molly had seen her husband taken to prison before, and she did not realise that this was a much more serious affair than were his poaching misdemeanours, so that she was not so much overpowered as might have been expected; and, as he was taken by the well-known constable instead of the soldiers, she did not treat it as John's fault. Besides, she was really afraid of, as she said, "upsetting" Judith by another outcry, so she only moaned in a low, miserable voice about what was to become of her and her poor children, though after all, what with the parish, Judith's help, and John's earnings, she would be no worse off than was common with her. Jem was supposed to "keep himself," and only Judy was really on her hands.

She would hardly let her son go up and see Judith. "Now, you'll be terrifying of her, and she'll be upset again and holler, and go into a fit."

However, he took off his boots and went up softly. Judith was all alone, lying still, but he had never seen her look half so ill, though she opened her eyes and smiled when the creaking stair announced him, and when he bent over her she said, "Dear lad, you bain't hurt!"

"Oh no; not at all."

"And the dear ladies are safe?"

"Yes; Tirzah Todd came and took them away."

"Thank God!"

"But you are bad, auntie?"

"Oh, never mind. All's right! You've done your duty, and I can only thank God for my good lad."

Her voice grew faint, her eyes closed, and John was obliged to go away — but the look of peace stayed with him.

Chapter XXV.

Judith.

"And of our scholars let us learn
Our own forgotten lore."
Keble.

Little Mary Carbonel was not the worse for all the agitations, from which, indeed, she had been so carefully shielded, but her mother was sadly broken down by all she had undergone, and likewise by mortification at the whole conduct of the Uphill people. After all the years that she and her husband and sisters had striven for them, it was very hard to find that so very few would exert themselves for their protection, and that so many would even turn against them. It was hard to make allowance for the bewilderment of slow minds, for sheer cowardice, and for the instinct of going along with one's own class of people. She and Sophy prayed that they might forgive the people, but it was impossible just then not to feel that there was a good deal to forgive, and Captain Caiger was always telling them that all their trouble came in trying to help the good-for-nothing people.

They had moved into the George Hotel at Elchester. It was a good large inn, such as used to exist in coaching days, where travellers stopped for meals, and sometimes spent a night, and the rooms were so comfortable that they were glad to stay there, while Captain Carbonel could go backwards and forwards to make arrangements about the repair of Greenhow. Of course, when he came to look the place over with a builder from Elchester it turned out that a great deal more was needed than simply rebuilding what had been burnt; and he was in difficulties about the cost, when an offer came which he was glad to accept.

The Seven Ionian Islands had been put under the protection of England since they had been set free from the Turkish dominion, and the Governor, Sir Thomas Maitland, (King Tom as he was often called), was very active in building, making roads, and improving them in every way possible. He wanted an English officer to superintend his doings in the little isle of Santa Maura, and being acquainted with Major Sandford, Dora's husband, the proposal was made that Captain Carbonel should undertake the work for two or three years, bringing out, of course, his family with a handsome salary. It was a most opportune offer, giving him the means of renewing Greenhow, of a visit to the sister, and of restoring his wife's health, which had been much tried by her child's death, little Mary's delicate state, and the alarm of the riots. So it was gladly accepted, and the departure was to take place as soon as the trials were over, for a special commission had been appointed to try the rioters; and poor Sophy was much distressed at having so evidently recognised Dan Hewlett when she found that "rioting and arson," that is, burning, made a capital offence, so that it was a matter of life and death.

But there was another to whom this same discovery made a great difference — namely, Dan Hewlett himself. When he found that his life was at stake, he declared himself willing to turn King's evidence, if his pardon were secured to him, and this was really important, as he was able to identify Jack Swing, who really was the chief mischief-maker, being a young clerk whose head had been turned by foolish notions about liberty for the people, and who really acted more generously, and with less personal spite, than most of his unhappy followers. However, Dan was content to purchase his own life by denouncing the leader whom he had followed, and he was promised safety after the trial should be over, until which time he must remain in prison at Minsterham.

Captain Carbonel had consulted George Hewlett, when arranging the ruins at Greenhow, as to what had best be done for John, whose services he could not forget. George considered for a night, and the next day said —

"Well, sir, I beg your pardon, but the best thing as could be done with that there John would be to put him somewhere to learn the cabinet-making. He is a right sharp, clever hand, and knows pretty well all I can teach him; and he would get on famous if he had the chance. And it bain't so comfortable for him here. Some of 'em owes him a grudge for bringing the soldiers down on 'em, and calls him an informer; and it will be all the worserer for him when his father comes home — the scamp that he is! I'm ready to wish my name wasn't the same. Wuss shame by far than to be strung up to turn agin him as he was hand and glove with!"

"I am quite of your opinion, Hewlett; and I fully think John would be best out of the way, poor fellow. I will inquire for a good master for him."

"Thank you, sir. I would have had the boy up to sleep at my place, but he won't leave his poor aunt. He be the chief comfort she has, poor thing. But she won't be here long anyway; and if ever there was a good woman, 'tis Judith Grey."

It was quite true. Mr. Harford, who had come home on Saturday, walked over to Poppleby, partly for the sake of saying that Judith was certainly near the close of her trials, and that it was her great wish to see one of the dear ladies again, though she durst not ask one of them to come into Dan's house. Indeed Mr. Harford had only drawn the expression of her desire out of her with difficulty.

Mrs. Carbonel was not well enough for a trying interview, so it was Sophy who drove from Elchester with her brother-in-law, grave and thoughtful, and only wishing to avoid everybody; for she could not yet forget how no one had shown any gratitude, nor desire to shield those who had been so long their friends. The Poppleby doctor had been sent to see Judith, and had pronounced that the old disease had made fatal progress, accelerated by the hysterical convulsions caused by the night and day of suspense and anxiety, and the attack on her nephew, as well as the whole of Dan's conduct. He did not think that she could last many more days.

So Sophy arrived at the well-known cottage, and was met at the door by Molly, with her apron to her eyes, and a great deal to say about her poor sister, and "it wasn't her wish"; but Mr. Harford, who was on the watch, began to answer her, so as to keep her from going upstairs with the visitors. Little Judy, now a nice, neat girl of fourteen, was sitting by her, but rose to go away when the lady came in.

Judith was leaning against pillows, and the pink flush in her cheeks and her smile of greeting prevented Sophy from seeing how ill and wasted she looked, thin and weak as were the fingers that lay on the coverlet.

"Why, Judith, you look much better than I expected. You will soon be as well as ever."

Judith only smiled, and said, "Thank you, ma'am! I hope Mrs. Carbonel is better."

"Yes. She is getting better now, and she is very sorry not to come and see you; but perhaps she may be able before we go away."

"And little Miss Mary, ma'am?"

"She has been quite another creature since we have been at Poppleby — not at all fretty, and almost rosy."

"I am glad. And you are going away, ma'am?"

"Yes; off to a beautiful island in the Mediterranean Sea, close to all the places where Saint Paul preached. You know Dora is at Malta, where he was shipwrecked."

"Yes, ma'am; I like to know it. You will give my duty to her, Miss Sophy, and thank her — oh! so much," — and Judith clasped her hands — "for all she and you and Mrs. Carbonel have been to me. You seemed to bring the light back to me, just as my faith was growing slack and dull."

"Yes; I will tell her, Judith. I don't like leaving you, but it won't seem long till we come back; and we will send you those beautiful Maltese oranges."

Judith smiled that beautiful smile again. "Ah, Miss Sophy, you have been very good, and helped me ever so much; but my time is nearly over, and I shall not want even you and madam where I am going. I shall see His face," she murmured; and lifted up her hands.

Sophy was rather frightened, and felt as if she had done wrong in talking of oranges. She did not know what to say, and only got out something about Johnnie and a comfort.

"Yes, that he is, Miss Sophy, and little Judy too. The boy, he is that shy and quiet, no one would believe the blessed things he says and reads to me at night. He be a blessing, and so be Judy, all owing to the Sunday School."

"Oh! to you, Judith. You made him good before we had him, though Mary and Dora did help," said Sophy, with rising tears.

"And oh! I am so thankful," she said, clasping her hands, "for what the captain is doing for the boy."

"He deserves it, I am sure," said Sophy.

"It will keep him easier to the right way, and it would be harder for him when I am gone, and his father come home! And Mr. Harford, he says he will find a good place for Judy. She is a good girl, a right good girl."

"That she is."

"And, maybe, Mrs. Carbonel and you, when you come home, would be good to my poor sister. She've been a good sister to me, she has, with it all, but it has all been against her, and she would be a different woman if she could. Please remember her."

"We will, we will if we can."

Then Judith went on to beg Sophy to write to her former mistress, Mrs. Barnard, with all her thanks for past kindness. That seemed to exhaust her a good deal, and she lay back, just saying faintly, "If you would read me a little bit, miss."

The Prayer-Book lay nearest, and Sophy read, "Lord, now lettest Thou Thy servant depart in peace," as well as she could amid the choking tears. She felt as if she were lifted into some higher air, but Judith lay so white and still that she durst not do more than say, "Good-bye, dear Judith." She was going to say, "I will come and see you again," but something withheld her. She thought Judith's lips said, "Up there." She bent down, kissed the cheek, now quite white, and crept down, passing Molly at the turn.

Two days later Mr. Harford came to say that Judith was gone. Her last communion with Johnnie, and with George Hewlett, had been given to her the day before, and she had not spoken afterwards, only her face had been strangely bright.

The Carbonels could only feel that her remnant of life had been shortened by all she had undergone for their sakes, and Edmund and Sophy both stood as mourners at her grave,

Sophy feeling that her life had been more of a deepening, realising lesson than anything that had gone before, making her feel more than had ever come yet into her experience, what this life is compared with eternal life.

Chapter XXVI.

The Golden Chains.

"A form unseen is pulling us behind,
Threads turn to cords, and cords to cables strong,
Till habit hath become as Destiny,
Which drives us on, and shakes her scourge on high."
Isaac Willia s.

Captain Carbonel lost no time after Judith Grey's funeral in sending John Hewlett to his new master, Mr. Jones. The place was the Carbonels' old home, in a county far-away from Uphill. George had wished the lad to go to a cabinet-maker whom he knew at Minsterham, but he was convinced by the captain's advice to let him be quite away from the assizes, which would not only be pain and shame to him, but would mark his name with the brand of the same kind as that of an informer. This Mr. Jones was well-known to the Carbonel family as an excellent man — a churchwarden, and sure to care for the welfare, spiritual as well as bodily, of those commended to him.

And it happened, not unfortunately for John, that, in the captain's handwriting, his rather uncommon name was read as Newlett, and for some time after he arrived he never found out the mistake, and was rather glad of it when he did so, since no one connected him with the rick-burner who gave evidence against his leader.

Dan himself came home to find that he was held in more utter disgrace than for all his former disreputable conduct, which only passed for good-fellowship. If he had been hanged, or even transported, he would only have been "poor Dan Hewlett," and his wife would have had all the pity due to widowhood; but everybody fought shy of him, and the big lads hooted at him. He could not get work, Judith's pension had failed, and they lived scantily on what Farmer Goodenough allowed Molly to earn, as an old hand, to be kept off the parish. Little Judith was apprenticed to Mrs. Pearson, according to the old fashion which bound out pauper girls as apprentices to service, and which had one happy effect, namely, that they could not drift foolishly from one situation to another, though, in bad hands, they sometimes had much to suffer. But Mrs. Pearson was a kind, conscientious mistress, and Judy was a good girl, so that all went well.

Dan slouched about, snared rabbits and hares, and drank up the proceeds thereof at little public-houses where he was not known, or where the company was past caring about his doings. At last, he was knocked down in the dark by the mail-coach, and brought home in a cart, slowly dying.

Mr. Harford came to see him, and found his recollections of old times reviving, when he had been Dame Verdon's best scholar. "I could beat old George any day at his book. And, then, I was church singer, and had the solos," he said, evidently thinking sadly of his better days. "And my wife, she was that tidy — only she did put too much on her back!"

The screen, which Judith had of late years kept with the panel with the laburnums on the back side, had by accident been now turned so that he saw them; and, when Mr. Harford came the next day, he broke out —

"Them flowers! Them flowers, sir!"

Mr. Harford could not understand.

"Them golden chains, sir. They was at the bottom of it."

Mr. Harford understood still less.

"They talk of devils' chains, sir, and how they drags a man down. Them was a link, sure enough. That paper there, sir, I keeps seeing it at night by the rushlight, and they gets to look just like chains."

Then Mr. Harford understood that he meant the laburnums on the paper — golden chains, as they are often called.

"I was working with George," he said, "before them Carbonels came, and when there was a piece of the parlour paper left over, I took it for a parkisit. I didn't let George know; he always seemed too particular. 'Twas more than I had reckoned on; and one bit I papered Mrs. Brown's room, at Downhill, with; and one bit that was left my wife put on the screen. Then, when the captain made a work about it, I thought it was mean and shabby in him, and I never could lay my mind to him or his after that — special after Miss Sophy came and spied it out. I went agen 'em more and more, and all they wanted for the place; and it riled me the more that my lad should be took up with them and his aunt. And so the ill-will of it went on with me, worse and worserer. Molly, I say, take the devils' chains away. They've got a hold of me."

That was his delirious cry. Mr. Harford prayed with him and for him, but never could tell how much was remorse and how much might be repentance. He was quieter as his strength failed, and his wife said he made a beautiful end, and that she was sure the Holy Name of the Saviour was on his lips, and Mr. Harford trusted that she was right, with the charity that hopeth all things.

Chapter XXVII.

Missed and Mourned.

"Nor deem the irrevocable Past
As wholly wasted, wholly vain."
Longfellow.

"Be they Gobblealls not coming home?" asked Nanny Barton, as she stood at her gate, while some of her neighbours came slowly out of church, about two years later.

"My man, he did ask Shepherd Tomkins," said Betsy Seddon, "and all the answer he got was, 'You don't desarve it, not you.' As if my man had gone out with that there rabble rout!"

"And I'm sure mine only went up to see what they were after, and helped to put out the fire beside."

"Ay," said Cox, behind her, "but not till the soldiers were come."

"Time they did come!" said Seddon. "Rain comes through the roof, and that there Lawyer Brent won't have nothing done to it till the captain comes home."

"Yes," added Morris, "and when I spoke to him about my windows, as got blown in, he said 'cottages were no end of expense, and we hadn't treated them so as they would wish to come back nohow.'"

"Think of their bearing malice!" cried Nanny Barton.

"I don't believe as how they does," responded the other Nanny. "They have sent the coals and the blankets all the same."

"Bear malice!" said Mrs. Truman, who had just walked up. "No, no. Why, Parson Harford have said over and over again, when he gave a shilling or so or a meat order, to help a poor lady that was ill, that 'twas by madam's wish."

"And Governess Thorpe, she has the bag of baby-linen and half a pound of tea for any call," said Mrs. Spurrell.

"But one looks for the friendly word and the time of day,"

sighed Betsy Seddon.

"The poor children, they don't half like their school without the ladies to look in," said Mrs. Truman. "It is quite a job to get them there without Miss Sophy to tell them stories."

"I can't get mine to go at all on Sundays," said Nanny Morris.

"And," added Betsy Seddon, "I'm right sure my poor Bob would never have 'listed for a soldier if the captain had been at home to make Master Pucklechurch see the rights of things, and not turn him off all on a suddent."

"Master Pucklechurch, he don't believe they are never coming back," said Widow Mole, who had just come that way as an evening walk with her children. "He says little miss, and madam too, have their health so much better out there, that they won't like to come home. And yet they have made the place like a picture. I was up there to help Sue Pucklechurch clean it up, and 'tis just a pleasure to see all the new outhouses and sheds, as you might live in yourself, and well off too."

"And that it should all be for them Pucklechurches," sighed Seddon.

"I heerd tell," said Mrs. Truman, "that Lawyer Brent was to come and live in the house, and that was why they are making it so nice."

On this there arose a general wail of lamentation, and even of indignation. Nobody loved Lawyer Brent, who was a hard, if a just, man, anxious for his employer's good, but inclined, in spite of all cautions, to grind the tenants. To hear of his coming to Greenhow was dismal news to all concerned, and there was such a buzz of doleful inquiries that Mr. Harford stopped on his way home to ask what was the matter.

"Oh no," he said, when he heard. "Captain and Mrs. Carbonel are coming home in the spring, only they wished to travel slowly, so as to see something of foreign parts. You need not be afraid. We shall have them back again, and I hope nobody will be as foolish as before. I am sure they have quite forgiven."

And, on a fine spring day, the bells were ringing at the church, and everybody stood out at the cottage doors, curt-

seying and bowing with delight and welcome; and Mrs. Carbonel and Miss Sophia and Miss Mary, looking rosy, healthy,
and substantial, and even little Master Edmund was laughing
and nodding, and looking full of joy. While the captain walked
up with Mr. Harford, and greeted every one with kindly,
hearty words. No one could doubt that they were glad to be at
home again, and after all that had come and gone, that they
felt that these were their own people whom they loved.

Chapter XXVIII.

Conclusion.

"The work be Thine, the fruit Thy children's part."
— *Keble.*

Look at Uphill Priors in the year 1880. Here are the mothers coming out of the mothers' meeting. They look, in their neat hats and jackets, better on this weekday than any one would have done on Sunday sixty years ago. They are, many of them, the granddaughters, or grandsons' wives, of the inhabitants in those old times; but they have not the worn, haggard faces that their parents had when far younger, except one or two poor things who have drunken husbands. Miss Carbonel (young Miss Carbonel) and the vicar's wife have been working with them, and reading to them things that the Bettys and Nannys of those days would not have understood or cared for.

The white-haired lady, who stops her donkey-chaise to exchange some affectionate, kindly words, and give out a parcel or two — she is Miss Sophia; and those elderly women who cluster round for a greeting, they are her old scholars. Those black eyes are Hoglah's; that neat woman is Judy! Yes, she has lived among them, and worked among them all her life, never forgetting that "no good work can be done without drudgery." She has her Girls' Friendly Society class still in her own little house, though she has dropped most of her regular out-of-door work of late years. For the vicar — there is a vicar now — and his daughters teach constantly in the schools. The children are swarming out now, orderly and nice, even superior in appearance to some of the mothers they run up to; and as to learning, the whole parish can read and write, and the younger ones can send out a letter that would be no disgrace to a lady or a gentleman.

There is a machine, with its long tail of spikes, coughing along as it blows off the steam at Farmer Goodenough's. No one dreams of meddling with it to do any harm. Wages are better, food is cheaper, and there are comforts in the house of every one tolerably thrifty that the grandmothers look at as novelties. John and George Hewlett, carpenters and builders, have a handsome shop and large workshop in the street.

All this has come in the way of gradual change, brought about not by rioting, but by the force of opinion, and the action of those in authority.

But how have people been fitted to make a good use of these things — not to waste them, but to use them as God's good gifts? There has been a quiet influence at work ever since "they Gobblealls" came up the roughness of the lanes, and "Mary's approach" was given up.

Captain Edmund, and Mary his wife, lie in their quiet graves, but the work they did — by justice, by kindness, by teaching, by example — has gone on growing, and Miss Sophia looks at it, and is thankful, as she still gives her best in love and experience to the young generation who are with her and look up to her for help and counsel.

The church is beautiful now, not only to look at, nor merely in the well-performed music of the services, but in the number and devotion of the worshippers and communicants. Of course, all is not perfect in the place — never, never will it be so in this world; but the boys and youths can, and often are, saved from a fit of thoughtless heathenism by their clubs and their guilds, and the better families are mostly communicants. Blots there are, and the vicar sometimes desponds when some fresh evil crops up; but Miss Sophia always tells him to hope, and that —

"The many prayers, the holy tears, the nurture in the Word,
Have not in vain ascended up before the Gracious Lord."

Finis.